D1040448

Feb 2016

THE POPE'S
DAUGHTER

Dario Fo

THE POPE'S DAUGHTER

*Translated from the Italian
by Antony Shugaar*

Europa
editions

Europa Editions
214 West 29th Street
New York, N.Y. 10001
www.europaeditions.com
info@europaeditions.com

Library of Congress Cataloging in Publication Data is available
ISBN 978-1-60945-274-2

Fo, Dario
The Pope's Daughter

Book design by Emanuele Ragnisco
www.mekkanografici.com
Illustration drawn and painted by Dario Fo
in collaboration with Jessica Borroni and Michela Casiere.
Cover image: illustration by Dario Fo.
Photo by Luca Vittorio Toffolon.

Prepress by Grafica Punto Print – Rome

Printed in the USA

THE POPE'S DAUGHTER

Proscenium

"God! Seen from above and stark naked, you're even handsomer!
To what house do you belong, Neapolitan?"
—Lucrezia to Alfonso of Aragon

"In the production we saw, there were children on the proscenium, and at the height of the most tasteless and grotesque of the pantomimes, they could do nothing more than look on in horror."
—LUCREZIA TO HER BROTHER CESARE

CONTENTS

PREAMBLE

Lucrezia

Jumping feet-first into the mud

Concerning the lives, the triumphs, and the misdeeds of the Borgias, and based on the more or less thorough and accurate documentation thereof, operas and plays have been written and staged, noteworthy films have been made starring renowned actors, as well as, most recently, two remarkably popular television series.

What is the explanation of our enduring interest in the doings of these individuals? Undoubtedly it is the shameless lack of any moral compass that they are said to have displayed at every turn in their story. A way of life without restraint, be it in matters sexual or affairs of state and society.

Among the great writers who have recounted the dramatic deeds, deep-seated cynicism, and torrid love affairs of this powerful clan, we should mention Alexander Dumas, *père*, Victor Hugo, Maria Bellonci, and Rafael Sabatini. But one of the most renowned is John Ford, an Elizabethan playwright writing at the turn of the seventeenth century. He wrote and staged *'Tis Pity She's a Whore*, a play almost certainly based on the alleged exploits of Lucrezia Borgia and her brother Cesare, who were long rumored to have been incestuous lovers. Our good friend Margherita Rubino has researched the theatrical works written during the lives of the Borgias and has identified not one but two playwrights—Giovanni Falugi and Sperone Speroni—who drew on this story, disguising

Francesco Sforza

Ludovico the Moor

it by giving it an ancient Roman provenance, allegedly from Ovid.

Undoubtedly, if we remove the story of Pope Alexander VI and his family from its context in Renaissance Italy, what we get is a shocking saga in which all the leading characters act without regard for their adversaries and quite often each other.

At every twist and turn, the victim destined for sacrifice, ever since she was a child, is Lucrezia. It is she who is tossed into the gaping maw of financial and political interests by both her father and her brother, without a qualm. What the lovely young maiden might think or feel is of no concern. After all, she's just a female, a judgment that came as easily to her father, the future pope, as to her brother, soon to be made cardinal. In fact, there are points in the narrative when Lucrezia seems to be nothing more than a package of shapely breasts and a magnificent derrière. Ah, we almost forgot, her eyes too were twin pools of enchantment.

Still, the horrors in Italy did not unfold so spectacularly only in the milieu of Rome. Let us examine another instance, the court of Milan, where we will make the acquaintance of the Viscontis and the Sforzas, who'll appear frequently, often playing leading roles.

In 1447 Filippo Maria Visconti died without male issue, his only heir an illegitimate daughter, Bianca Maria; she was promptly legitimized so that she could be married off to Francesco Sforza, whose father, a soldier of fortune, was a commoner by birth. In fact, Francesco Sforza's grandfather was a miller. And voilà, the birth of a new dynasty. The young bride gave birth to eight sons and daughters, including Galeazzo Maria and Ludovico, who will be known as Ludovico the Moor.

Galeazzo Maria was, to use the phrase current in Neapolitan slang, a *sciupafemmene*, a lady killer, an unrepentant lothario as likely to frequent noblewomen as prostitutes. His behavior in fact won him numerous enemies, and when he was finally murdered it was at the hands of not one but several assassins. He was stabbed to death outside the church of Santo Stefano, and precisely on the name day of that church's titular saint, St. Stephen, that is, December 26, 1476, by Giovanni Andrea Lampugnani, Gerolamo Olgiati, and Carlo Visconti, better known as Il Bastardo. So many conspirators were in on the deed, like some latter-day Julius Caesar!

Upon Galeazzo Maria's death, the succession would ordinarily have fallen to his eldest child and only male heir, Gian Galeazzo, who was just seven. But Ludovico the Moor, with French support, took over as regent and quickly exploited his nephew's youth to strengthen and expand his own grip on power. But his criminal acts did not end here. Determined to rid himself once and for all of his young rival, who was also his nephew, he decided to poison him very slowly, little by little, in such a way that he could never be accused of his murder. The young man died, sure enough, after long drawn-out suffering, and his uncle Ludovico the Moor wept hot tears over his nephew's coffin, and then grabbed his inheritance, the duchy of Milan.

Why have we devoted so much space to this lordly lineage? Just to begin with, because a few years later Ludovico the Moor married Beatrice d'Este, whose brother Alfonso—Alfonso d'Este to be exact—would become one of Lucrezia Borgia's husbands. But that's not the only instance of family ties: Isabella d'Este, sister to Alfonso and Beatrice, later married Francesco Gonzaga, the Marchese of Mantua, and as we shall see, she too figures in some of the spicier gossip about Lucrezia. And if we look even closer, the circle still isn't complete.

In order that our readers fully appreciate the atmosphere in which people lived in Rome and all of Italy at the end of the fifteenth century, it would be useful, before proceeding, to recall a few other details. To this end, we may well profit by reading a letter that a young and newly consecrated bishop wrote to an old classmate from the seminary.

Elegant parties with lovely women

The prelate tells the tale of a papal orgy during which the *bonae femmene*, that is, the high-ranked courtesans invited to the ceremony, put on a dance competition in which they each performed a squatting curtsey, dropping their buttocks to the floor, where a line of scented candles stood burning. Each dancer, naturally after hiking her skirts, put out her candle and then rose again to a standing position, gripping the stub of candle with her vaginal muscles, taking great care not to let it fall. There was no shortage of applause.

Finally, one last noteworthy episode, which takes us all the way up to the threshold of our story: on July 23, 1492, Pope Innocent VIII fell into a coma, and his death was expected to occur within days.

Savonarola, the scourge of bishops and popes, had this to say about him: "[The pretext of] art is the same damnation that is now desecrating the throne of St. Peter in Rome [. . .]. We are talking about Pope Innocent VIII, in whose life the only thing that was ever innocent was his name."

And yet Alexandre Dumas, *père*, who wrote a magnificent history of the Borgias and the popes that preceded them, tells us that he was called "the father of his people," because thanks to his amatory energy he had increased the number of his subjects by eight sons and eight daughters in a life spent indulging in the voluptuous arts—all with different lovers, of course. It is not known how he chose those lovers because, it is well known, he suffered from a catastrophic case of myopia. In fact,

went and, with every person he met, to whisper the name, the
sex, the age, and the physical appearance of whoever was kiss-
ing the papal ring at that moment.

Still, it has to be admitted that this sinner-pope had an elevated sense of family. The care he showed for his children
should be considered acts of love rather than unworthy exam-
ples of nepotism.

In fact he selected just the right broodmares for the task at
hand—the task of propagating his family—from among the
daughters of powerful and illustrious men, beginning with the
beloved infanta of Lorenzo de' Medici who was married off to
his own firstborn son, Franceschetto Cybo. And there were
other young men from the most illustrious dynasties in Italy,
for his many daughters.

In his book *The Civilization of the Renaissance in Italy,*
Jacob Burckhardt describes a number of the more interesting
aspects of the behavior of Innocent VIII and his son
Franceschetto: the father-and-son pair, he writes, "established
an office for the sale of secular favors, in which pardons for
murder and manslaughter were sold for large sums of money.
Out of every fine, 150 ducats were paid into the papal exchequer,
and what was over, to Franceschetto. Rome, during the latter
part of this pontificate, swarmed with licensed and unlicensed
assassins."

Clemency and indulgences are a safeguard of power

But what especially catches our attention is that to this
already substantial group of rogues and scoundrels were added
another two hundred, possibly more, in that July of 1492. It
may seem incredible, but that's exactly what happened: that
month, there were more than two hundred murder victims,

Pope Innocent VIII

meaning there were just as many murderers. Two hundred! In just a few weeks, one after the other, after the other.

How on earth could such an immense massacre happen?

It's easy enough to explain: in Rome, every time a pope died, there was a host of murders because in time-honored tradition, once the conclave elected a new pope, an amnesty was declared for anyone who might have committed a crime during the days of the interregnum.

So anyone nursing a murderous grudge took advantage of the papal vacancy to satisfy his thirst for vendetta, murdering whomever he chose, confident that he would be set free in a matter of days, and all thanks to the certainty of a sure and plenary indulgence. Good times!

And now that we have given a clear picture of the atmosphere that reigned, it is precisely from this death of a pope, and from what took place in the immediate aftermath, that we shall begin.

PART ONE

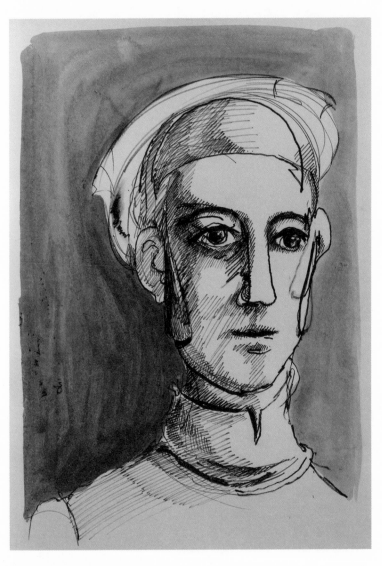

Rodrigo Borgia

The blessed lottery

On August 11, 1492, the artillery of Castel Sant'Angelo were fired to remind Rome and the world at large that a new pontiff had been elected, under the name of Alexander VI. At last Spain could lay claim to her second pope, Rodrigo Borgia.

In Rome a Pasquinade penned by the usual suspect exclaimed: "The papal throne has gone to the one who paid the most to those who run the holy lottery."

The Romans knew every cardinal in that lottery by Christian name and family affiliation: Ascanio Sforza, the brother of Ludovico the Moor, who had actually been given a city as a reward for his support, the city of Nepi, as well as four mules heavily laden with gold; Giuliano della Rovere, who was given assurances that it would be his turn to climb to the tip of the pyramid on the next go-round; and so on, with other gifts and prebends for all the other electors.

But now let us begin with this new pope, whose family we have chosen as the chief protagonists of our story.

Very little is known about the first Borgias and what scanty information has come down to us is insufficient to determine the family's origin; an origin that the flatterers and adulators of the Spanish dynasty actually traced back to the royal house of Aragon, a descent that seems highly unlikely.

In truth, the birth of this house can only be linked back to the authentic founder of the name, or perhaps we should say clan: we're talking about Alfonso Borgia. His father is sometimes called Domenico or Domingo, and at others Juan, while we don't even know his mother's surname.

Alfonso was born in Valencia in 1378. He was hired as a private scrivener to the royal court of Aragon, but with an astonishing change of headgear, we find him a short while thereafter in the robes of the bishop of Valencia. It was in that garb that he landed in Naples in the entourage of King Alfonso of Aragon, who became the monarch of Naples. Alfonso Borgia was made a cardinal in 1444. A rapid and astounding career!

It was a well-known fact: what Spain had in mind, and had been working to achieve since the middle of the fifteenth century, in rivalry with France, was to gain control of the papacy and full sway over Europe. And it was none other than the Borgias who began the conquest of the papal throne. To be precise, Alfonso was the first pontiff of the House of Borgia, and he donned the papal tiara in 1455 under the name of Callixtus III. On the heels of that pontiff, a forerunner to all that would follow, a considerable number of blood and acquired relatives of the Holy Father moved to Rome from Valencia. Among them was his favorite nephew: Rodrigo.

All of the many chroniclers and historians of the Borgias agree that Rodrigo came to Rome at the age of roughly eighteen, eager to place himself under the protection of the Spanish pontiff. This is just the first sign of the shameless nepotism of this high prelate, who gladly footed the bill for all the expenses the young man faced. Rodrigo had as his personal instructor none other than Maestro Gaspare da Verona, a man of great learning and extraordinary skill as a teacher.

Not long after that, the young man went to Bologna to study the law. The course of studies required for this degree was expected to take seven years. We should not assume that he plunged headfirst into the codices, enriching himself with nuggets of rhetoric and theology. The young man immediately won a great reputation among his classmates as a likable and respected individual. Rodrigo was an energetic student, handsome to behold and an eloquent and witty companion. He was beloved by young women and generous with his friends. He was therefore promptly elevated to the rank of ringleader of that gang of sons of the nobility and of the merchant class.

He faithfully attended all his lessons and was punctual in taking all his exams, which he passed with flying colors. But he also never missed a gathering of his fellow students, in both taverns and bordellos. "It's very difficult for a woman," his professor of rhetoric used to say, "to resist his courtship. He attracts women the way a magnet attracts iron filings. *Ferrum*, of course, is Latin for iron, and it sounds very much like another Latin word, *phallum*. Oh, my goodness, what have you made me say!"

On August 9, 1456, even though he had not yet completed the entire course of study, Rodrigo was allowed for special merits to take the final exam for his degree. His uncle, pleased and proud and in the meantime elevated to the papal throne, rewarded him by appointing him cardinal. Of course, that appointment was made discreetly and with great nonchalance, obviously to keep from triggering new charges of nepotism and favoritism.

But the special privileges did not end here. Callixtus III, now pope but still his uncle, decided to appoint his protégé the papal vicar to the March of Ancona. This was no easy task, because the warlords of the Marches were in revolt against the rule of Rome and at the same time in continual battle amongst themselves.

The youthful cardinal Rodrigo Borgia arrived in the city

with a small entourage of assistants, by night, and called a meeting for early the following morning in the palace of the curia of all those in charge of enforcing law and order in that city, as well as those in charge of collecting the taxes.

"I am here at the behest of the Holy Father," he introduced himself. "First of all I want to hear from you how you are faring in terms of enforcement, by which I mean how many arms-bearing men are at your disposal, and how many horsemen, and whether you have firearms, starting with your cannon. How many do you possess?"

The answer came shyly: "No, Your Eminence, we are still waiting for them but till now we haven't received any at all."

"That's fine, I've seen to it myself. I've brought with me four wagons with arquebuses, culverins, and muskets on tripods, because of the recoil, and there are four more teams of oxen hauling four cannons firing seven-pound shot."

"But we have no idea of how to use ordnance of that kind," humbly confessed the chief of guards.

"That is precisely why I am here."

"Will you instruct us yourself, Your Eminence?"

"I certainly could, but I'd prefer that you be taught by the two arquebus instructors I've brought with me."

"Forgive us, but do you intend to fire those guns?"

And the papal vicar replied: "I understand that—given the situation that has been developing in this magnificent city of yours, Ancona—you feel a certain restraint when it comes to firing bullets and cannonballs at the most eminent citizens of your city. I've asked around, and I understand that in this sometimes bloody dispute between noble factions, your representatives of law and order have always remained cautiously balanced—in a state of stable, unstable, and apparent equilibrium. In other words, you've put your own survival first and foremost, you sly dogs! But now you're going to have to make some hard choices. No more back-scratching, no more trading favors, no more turning a blind eye. You can't put it off any longer, now you have the resources you need to establish order: learn to shoot, or we'll turn these weapons on you."

"How would you do it? Who would do the firing?"

"In Rome I have a thousand men standing ready and, at a word from me, they can be here in just one day's march, ready to replace you, naturally after having given Christian burial to all those among you who might have refused our orders. The choice is up to you."

"But you see . . . We have had to give way to the relentless tyranny of these riotous lordlings, and they are armed . . . "

"Excuse me, but have you ever heard this name: Grippo dei Malatempora?"

"Yes," the corps of guards replied in chorus, "he's one of the notables who organized the last revolt!"

"Well, he is no longer a threat."

"Is he dead!?"

"No, he's a guest in your prisons. That's why I arrived by night with a group of men large enough to chain him up and cart him away. This bogeyman of yours will soon be on his way to Rome, and there he'll be tried and convicted straightaway. Do you like the word 'straightaway'?"

"Yes, indeed."

"Well, you can expect to hear it again many times while I'm here."

And so, for the first time, cannons and culverins were heard thundering in the city of Ancona.

We should say that those blasts had an extraordinary effect on the men in charge of the public administration. Rodrigo Borgia, the papal vicar in the March of Ancona, succeeded in capturing a hundred or so town notables and their henchmen. Casualties were minimal, relative to the value of that operation. A nice clean little job, in other words.

In the end, as he was about to mount his steed and ride away, in the presence of the city's authorities, both those who were handcuffed and those who were provisionally free, the papal vicar concluded his mission: "From this day forth your responsibilities to collaborate with the Papal State and His Holiness the Pontiff will no longer be a mere formality, they will now be explicit and effective. Therefore none of you, whether he be gonfalonier, captain of the people, or judge, will any longer be authorized to impose taxes, declare wars with sacking and plunder, sit in judgment, administer gambling or prostitution, coin money, or extort merchants, shopkeepers, and artisans like so many government usurers, as you have always done in the past. Ah, I was almost forgetting, each of you and the rest of the working population will have to provide proof each month that you have paid taxes to the Papal State that I represent."

It was a highly successful visit, especially as far as the populace was concerned, and in fact when the time came for him to say, "Farewell, we'll see each other again soon," the crowd followed him to the main gate, applauding and cheering and roaring out: "Hurry back, Rodrigo! We need someone like you!"

And there were a few who cried: "That's who they should make pope: you!"

"Thanks, I was just thinking the same thing, I'll do everything I can to make sure that happens," the cardinal replied, and then urged his horse on into a brisk trot.

When he reached Rome, many there had heard about what had happened in Ancona and most of them applauded his actions. Even the pontiff himself shamelessly applauded his behavior when he reached the Vatican, and embraced him like his own son. As a reward, he named him vice-chancellor, which amounted to saying that from that day forward the young man was second only to the pope himself.

What a career!

An ideal family

In those days, Rodrigo had one and possibly many amorous relationships. That lover, or those lovers, gave him three children. It may well be that it was only one woman, who became pregnant three different times; we're certainly not about to start nitpicking.

Relations with his uncle were close and constant and increasingly affectionate. But to his dismay, three years after being elected pontiff, Pope Callixtus III was laid low with a bad case of gout which the physicians declared to be life-threatening. No one suspected that frequenting ladies of the day or the night at that age might lead to such a malady. At any rate, this was the diagnosis of sixteenth-century medicine: the effects caused by the lures of the flesh, whether consumed at table or in bed, were always deleterious!

Knowing that the pontiff lay at death's door, the Roman noblemen, who, for the three full years of his papacy, had been forced to swallow in silence the broadsides of nepotism toward an intolerable number of close relatives, both blood and acquired by marriage, were finally able to exact revenge for that vast array of abuse. The privileges that for years had been the appanage of the Spaniards were now about to return to their hands. The usurpers were about to pay.

And in fact, one after another, the Iberian lackeys, servants, and professional adulators immediately took to their heels, and Rodrigo was left alone to hear the Holy Father's last words. It is touching to see how constant the nephew was in attending the sick man's bedside; it's safe to say he never left the dying pope alone. He was certainly keenly aware that by remaining there, alone, in the open, he was running the risk of becoming the sole target of brutal vendettas. And yet the most powerful member of the college of cardinals not only remained, unflinching, by his onetime protector's sickbed, but he also took care not to react with deed or threat while his palazzo was being sacked and plundered by the henchmen of the Colonna and Orsini families. And when the pontiff was finally dead, those families undertook a full-fledged purge.

Just for starters, Rodrigo's younger brother Pedro Luis, who had been appointed Captain-General of the Church and prefect of the city, was forced to flee in disguise to escape a lynch mob the day before the pope died. But luck wasn't on that Pedro Luis's side, even if he was a Borgia! He fled to Civitavecchia, where he died soon afterward of malarial fever.

In contrast, while everyone in Rome who was either Spanish or had had anything to do with the Spanish was being slaughtered, no one dared to lay a hand on Rodrigo. He was untouchable, not so much because of any protection being afforded by the newly powerful, but because of his reputation as a peerless executive and his unequaled talent as vice-chancellor. Unbelievable: talent and intelligence still counted for something.

At that moment, on the day that his uncle Pope Callixtus III died, the young Borgia was twenty-seven years old. During the reigns of four consecutive pontiffs, he would occupy without interruption that same office, second in power only to the pope himself. Until the day he had to give up the position in order to don the papal tiara himself.

In 1466, or possibly 1467, Cardinal Rodrigo met someone whom we can safely say was destined to be the most important woman in his life. If for no other reason than that she, some short time later, would give birth to Lucrezia.

She was a beautiful Roman woman, probably of Lombard origins, tall, slender, and alluring. Above all, she was very intelligent, or she'd never have been able to so completely capture the attention of a man with so much experience and power.

Her name was Giovanna Cattanei, but she was known as

Vannozza Cattanei

Vannozza. When they met, Vannozza was about twenty, and Rodrigo was eleven years older than her. The cardinal took great care to keep that relationship a secret. He procured for his lover a more than fitting home where nearly every night, with great caution, he was able to pay her a visit. And yet in the society of that century it was quite accepted for a man of the church to carry on openly reckless relations with women of any and all social ranks and birth.

We therefore find ourselves in the presence of an unquestionable libertine, but one with a certain sense of shame. And if you like, you're welcome to call it priestly hypocrisy, as Molière does in his *Tartuffe*.

The truly noteworthy aspect, however, is that in contrast with all the other relationships he'd carried on before now, in this one the high prelate seemed to be seeking not so much adventure, but rather a sense of family. In fact, the four children that were born to this union would be tended to, beloved, and raised in an almost normal family setting. And because he himself could not personally play the part of the father of this family, the cardinal hired someone to do it for him. And he chose his man with subtlety and cunning.

His name was Giorgio de Croce, and by profession he was an apostolic secretary. Needless to say, that job at the Vatican had been procured for this pretend father by Rodrigo, the real father. And of course, Rodrigo had added a little extra to his salary for the job of being father. In turn, Rodrigo had to invent an identity of his own, and he came up with one that was absolutely plausible: he became the uncle. A likable, generous uncle, one who was extraordinarily affectionate with his nieces and nephews. In fact, he came to see them every night, with armfuls of gifts. And sure enough Vannozza set aside a modest bedroom in her home, a pied-à-terre, just like in the *pochades*, or perhaps we should refer to the stage sets for the *commedia dell'arte*. The husband/father leaves through one door, the uncle/cardinal comes in through another and, as night draws on and the lamps are dimmed (surprise surprise) and once the children have been hugged and kissed goodnight, he withdraws into his room to sleep but just a few moments later he slips stealthily out and climbs into the bed of the wife of the false and now-absent husband. From time to time, he even runs into one or another of the children who've come in search of Mamma because they've been having nightmares, but the good uncle calms them down, rocks them in his arms, carries them back to their own beds, and even sings them a lullaby. Then he toddles off to sing one to the mother, too.

To tell the truth, of all those roles the toughest one belonged to the false husband. Playing the character of father and husband only to disappear as soon as his boss shows up and stay away until dawn, and then, as his employer tiptoes away, undress and get back in bed is not exactly the most fun-filled role available. But when the pay is good and the job is secure, it's worth swallowing even the part of a scoundrel.

But just as in the *commedia all'improvvisa* that was beginning to be seen on stage around that time, there was an unexpected plot twist. All of a sudden the false husband and false father died. Was this an invented development? No, it was all too true. And so, after a fitting funeral for the rented parent, amidst prayers and tears, the time came to choose another false father. And this time they actually hired a man of letters, Carlo Canale, younger than his predecessor (and more or less the same age as mother Vannozza). Of course, he too enjoyed considerable benefits: he was well paid, and he was required only to take care of the very consolable widow and the children, in the role of preceptor. For which he was paid separately.

Canale quickly discovered that his new children were quite gifted, both in the scientific disciplines and in literature and poetry. In particular, the most versatile and receptive was certainly Lucrezia, who at the time was only six. She learned Latin

and Greek with surprising facility, easily memorizing frag-
ments of poetry and lyrics by the best known authors of literature and science.

Six more years went by, and now the day had come when
Pope Innocent VIII (whom we mentioned at the beginning, in
reference to his extraordinary collection of lovers and the
numerous progeny with which he was endowed by these holy
relationships) lay moaning on his deathbed.

It had been thirty-five years since the death of his uncle
Callixtus III, and it is safe to say that the selection of popes
who had occupied the throne of St. Peter since that day had
been the result of the handiwork and skilled management of
Rodrigo Borgia. And, as we were saying, his talent for moving
cards and serving the interests that mattered made him more
and more invaluable in his role as deputy pope.

After Pius II, Paul II, Sixtus IV and, of course, Innocent
VIII, Cardinal Borgia decided that the time had come to have
himself elected to the highest ecclesiastic office. Now there was
no point in continuing to play the role of the generous uncle
who arrived every evening at the home of his nieces and
nephews only to sneak away the next day at dawn. Since he
would soon be the master of the Holy See of Rome, he could
safely put out with the trash any gossip that was certain to
explode once word got out that the pope had children and a
morganatic wife.

Now, however, it was time to reveal the truth to his off-
spring. We have no documentation on this phase of the
process, but it is easy to imagine the words and the dialogue
that must have ensued at the instant of revelation. He probably gathered together his family and said: "My dear children,
your uncle will soon become pope." A chorus of cheers and
applause, hugs and kisses from all the children. But at this point,

what age are the little ones? The eldest, Juan, was eighteen, Cesare was sixteen, Lucrezia twelve, and the fourth child, Jofré, was ten.

Lucrezia, leaping into Rodrigo's arms, asked him: "But will we still be able to call you uncle, or must we add Your Holiness?"

Rodrigo took a deep breath and, after a moment, invited them all to sit down around him, including Vannozza and her husband, and then he told them the unbelievable truth: "No, you mustn't call me uncle anymore, because the truth is, I'm not your mother's brother, and Carlo Canale isn't her real second husband, and your late father wasn't really your father at all."

The children were all struck dumb, and Cesare asked: "Then if everyone here is a playactor, fictitious, just who are you?"

"I am your father, your own true father, the father of you all, and not merely the spiritual father, but your actual, carnal father, and I engendered you with your mother, the only real person here."

Cesare asked in a resentful voice: "And why did you go on telling us this lie for all these years?"

"Because the truth would have created a scandal: the deputy pope, which is what I have been until now, has a woman that he loved! He brought into the world with that woman four little children, all of them the apples of his eye! And for you, too, it would have been difficult to emerge from that experience unharmed."

Lucrezia burst into tears, and with her, so did her youngest brother: "But you always taught us that we shouldn't lie," the daughter sniffed, "that it is wrong to betray or defile the truth. And now you tell us that everything in our home was false, a trick. Our father lied when he took us in his arms, he lied when he lay down in bed with our mother, and so did he, our

Rodrigo Borgia (Pope Alexander VI)

preceptor, it was all a lie. What will we say to our friends, to the people who sarcastically ask us, 'How are your fathers today?'"

Rodrigo calmly replied: "Just answer them by asking: 'How are yours?' because let me assure you of one thing, in the Vatican and surrounding areas, there are very few legitimate sons and daughters, and perhaps almost as few truly married mothers. In any case, know that I have always loved you as my own children, and now at last I can love you in the clear light of day."

"But why only now?"

"Why, it's as simple as can be, my darlings. In a few days I will be elected to the very tip of the pyramid. A pyramid made up of thousands of men, some more powerful and some less, and each with his arms raised helping to uphold the construction. Those who support this pyramid must do so by balancing carefully, and if they waver or wobble they are soon crushed or expelled and quickly replaced by someone better suited and more astute. The only one who is never at risk of being squeezed out of the pyramid is the one who stands at the very tip-top, that is, the pope. Only death can remove him from office. And so, neither slander nor calumny, to say nothing of unutterable truths, will be able to touch me. And the same goes for you, who are my children. As I once learned from my professor of geometry, it is a dynamic equilibrium that is the true strength of faith. There are those who say that this is blasphemy, but I like it just fine the way it is!"

The story of an impossible love. Without a net

We forgot to tell you that, some time before giving his off-spring the news that he was their true father, Rodrigo had met a very young maiden whose extraordinary beauty was well-known throughout the Rome that most mattered. This young woman was Giulia Farnese.

Back then the Farnese family was not yet famous: that was something that would happen a few years later. Giulia grew up in the countryside near Capodimonte, but she had been finely educated in literature, dance, and even music. In fact she played the lute delightfully. She had just emerged from puberty when she first met Cardinal Borgia in Rome; he was busy organizing the dress rehearsal for his election as pope.

Meeting the young woman was a genuine lightning strike— the kind of bolt from the blue that shakes mountains down to their very foundations. Giulia's beauty was described by one and all with such fervor that Raphael himself decided to do a portrait of her, a painting that became very famous. For the cardinal it was love at first sight. He was fifty-eight, bulging not only with spiritual power but also excess fat, so much so that he had considerable difficulty embracing that young girl, just turned fourteen, an adorable nymphet.

But how could the elderly prelate succeed in managing this relationship? It would be taken care of by Adriana Mila, Rodrigo's cousin; at that moment she is the one discreetly pulling all the strings. What is more, Mila was Lucrezia's nurse and lived in the same quarters as her. The dishonest nurse took care to ward off all risk of scandal. In order to provide even further cover, she managed to ensure that Rodrigo's new interest became close friends with Lucrezia. This was at exactly the same time as Lucrezia found out that her affectionate uncle was actually her father: and when she discovered that her father was also her close friend's lover her astonishment and dismay spilled out beyond all bounds of despair.

Alas, Rodrigo was not yet officially pope and so he could not afford to impose his private follies on the rest of the realm. Therefore he was forced to take steps. He had two alternatives:

Giulia Farnese

either give up this maiden entirely or keep her and share her, at least for appearance's sake, with some official tutor, better still if a husband in name only. But, as an old proverb would have it, it's always better to wash your dirty laundry at the family home. The dishonest nurse did precisely that, offering her own son, Orsino Orsini, as the beaming spouse of the soon-to-be pontiff's blushing lover. A solution that was perfectly suited for home and for church! What's more, young Orsino was blind in one eye, so turning the other blind eye became all the easier! But there was no time to waste: Giulia was pregnant, by Rodrigo, of course . . . . It is no accident that the word *bishop* in the language of the ancient Christians was understood to mean "active and infallible." Perfect! In any case, how much better it was that the son could be born with a legitimate father.

In the meantime, Lucrezia was now keenly aware of every maneuver and trick played by her father and her nurse. But what could she do now? How should she behave? To tell the truth, every so often she felt a certain disgust, and she wished that she could talk about things with Cesare, the brother in whom she had always confided when things were at their hardest, but unfortunately he was at the University of Pisa. Lucrezia had been living for some time now with her nurse, a dishonest panderer, and she was quite sure that she shouldn't confide in her. So she decided she'd talk to her mother and went to see her in her venerable old palazzo.

As soon as Lucrezia mentioned her sense of unease, Vannozza threw her arms around her and Lucrezia burst into tears.

"Mother, I've discovered that my father has a relationship with a girl who's younger than me."

"Yes, I know," her mother confided in a small, faint voice. "I also know that the puppet master behind this affair is your cousin Adriana. I'd guessed immediately that he'd found himself another girlfriend and that, most of all, this time, he'd had his fill of me."

And she in turn burst into tears.

We mentioned at the beginning that the most notable episodes in the lives of the Borgias—and in particular those involving Rodrigo's uncle Callixtus III, Rodrigo himself, and his warrior son and cardinal, Cesare—failed to arouse anything more than a token wave of astonishment or indignation in the society of that time. To put it briefly, it was accepted and customary for sheer ruthlessness to be the order of the day, for the private affairs of high prelates (those of ecclesiastical rank up to and including the pontiff himself), to be considered routine, no matter how scandalous the details. In other words, the idea was that those who luxuriated in the most sordid sin were individuals more or less free of any blinkered, false sense of shame and were therefore, paradoxically, all the more trustworthy. The chronicles of the time, in fact, reported all sorts of social events, some of them held within the walls of the Vatican itself, with a matter-of-fact approach and without the slightest hint of scandal. But when the Borgias strode onto the stage of Renaissance history, to the cheers of a horde of supporters, first and foremost among them their closest relations, then indeed the attention of the public, an audience both national and international, really became keen.

And that attention was expressed not merely in the form of the so-called four-stanza Pasquinades, short compositions in rhyming verse; in fact jesters and satirical poets felt free to join in that game, bordering on calumny, often risking the ferocious retaliation of the Spanish political claque and of the Borgias themselves—the family was already notorious for the cruelty with which it punished its detractors.

The high point of creative embroidery in the fine art of scandalmongering came with the circulation of rumors concerning certain incestuous love affairs, to the point of insinuating that Lucrezia had been seduced by both her father, the prince of the church, and her brother, the pitiless warrior. It should be noted that there is no solid evidence of these outrageous acts. In that case, what testimony did the detractors bring to buttress their charges?

Marriage is the keystone that upholds the arch beneath which the most unsettling trysts thrive and prosper

Here we must begin with Lucrezia's marriage to Giovanni Sforza, the nephew of Ascanio Sforza, the powerful cardinal who was instrumental in securing Rodrigo Borgia's election to pope as Alexander VI.

It was an arranged marriage with starkly political ends. It was designed to strengthen the ties between the pope and Ludovico the Moor, who was in favor of inviting Charles VIII, the French king, to invade Italy in order to eliminate the annoying and dangerous power of Alfonso II of Aragon, king of Naples. On June 12, 1493, Lucrezia married the young scion of the Sforza family—he too was an illegitimate son. Attending the ceremony, to the enormous astonishment of the assembled crowd, was the bride's father, none other than the Holy Pontiff, surrounded by ten cardinals in full regalia. Among all those prelates, bedecked in purple and red, was also Lucrezia's brother, Cesare. But what was he doing in the midst of that crowd of high churchmen? Nothing could be simpler: just a few weeks earlier his father had named Cesare a cardinal too. Congratulations were in order!

With his attendance at that wedding the Borgia pope clearly meant to officially announce that Lucrezia was his beloved daughter, the fruit of his loins. Cesare wrapped his arms around his sister and hugged her so hard he lifted her off her feet; then he planted a kiss square on her lips, which produced an intense

Giovanni Sforza

*Cesare Borgia,
the Valentino*

buzz of commentary. There can be no doubt that her shameless brother meant to give her a sign of his undying love.

"Incestuous or not, there is no doubt that Cesare and Lucrezia loved each other above anyone else and remained loyal to each other to the end. Lucrezia was the only exception to Cesare's dismissal of women as irrelevant."[1]

During the wedding reception, at the appearance of each new celebrated guest, the *Oh!*'s of astonishment followed breathlessly one upon the other. Adding to this windstorm was the excitement that swept through the crowd when it became clear that the young woman sitting next to the pope was none other than Giulia Farnese, now widely acknowledged as his official favorite.

But, coming back to the festivities, Ludovico the Moor's wedding gift for the groom was the concession of sovereignty over the city of Pesaro. The pope threw in a dowry in the amount of 31,000 ducats. The union of the two young people, however, was not immediately consummated, because Lucrezia was still, so to speak, a mere fledgling: she was only thirteen. After the wedding her father took her away with him and in order to keep the bridegroom from becoming an annoyance he shipped him off to Pesaro. To make sure that everything went just as it ought to, the pope assigned his favorite son, Cesare, to keep an eye on him: the newlywed groom was already acquainted with Cesare's reputation as the pope's most ruthless servant.

It was only a few months later that Lucrezia was taken to Pesaro, so that the marriage could be consummated. But, please, with proper calm and respect.

---

[1] Sarah Bradford, *Lucrezia Borgia: Life, Love, and Death in Renaissance Italy,* Viking, New York 2004, p. 94.

Four years went by. The newlyweds were living peacefully, but in an atmosphere plagued with boredom. In fact, they were living in the provinces and, what's more, in the midst of a court devoid of spirit and initiative. Still, Giovanni behaved like a happy husband, deep in love. And why should he have not? We need only take a look at the renowned portrait of Lucrezia by Bartolomeo Veneto, where the young woman appears adorned by a crown of fine blonde hair that exalts the features of a face of astounding loveliness, and we are moved to exclaim: "No one on earth can escape the allure of such beauty."

But in the meanwhile, as by now had become customary, the Borgias' political ambitions suddenly shifted dramatically. Why on earth? What can have happened?

The puppet king who walks like a marionette

What had happened is that the young king of France Charles VIII decided to invade Italy with a mighty army, ignoring the more prudent opinions of his advisers. The twenty-two-year-old monarch—described by chroniclers as an obtuse megalomaniac, and called by some of his subjects *le roi guignol*, the puppet king, because of his puppetlike face and way of moving—intended to take for himself the kingdom of Naples, and to that end he had assembled an army of forty thousand men. His Italian allies were Ludovico the Moor, Giuliano della Rovere, and Ercole d'Este (whom we have yet to meet). It's a well-known fact that in Italy you practically can't turn around without bumping into people willing to climb onto the bandwagon of the first invader to happen by.

At this point, clashes began to break out all over. The Neapolitan fleet was defeated by the French naval forces, the papal army found itself surrounded in Romagna, and most

Lucrezia

crucial of all, the Orsinis and the Colonnas went over to the likely future masters of Italy. The pope realized that under those conditions, it was impossible to go on resisting the "*franzosi*." Alexander VI therefore decided to take shelter in the secure fortress of Castel Sant'Angelo and await more encouraging events.

And so Charles VIII made his triumphal entrance into the Eternal City, cheered on by the usual gang of henchmen and turncoats. The pope's first instinct was to take to his heels, but then deep-seated pride and a powerful sense of dignity took over. He decided to play all the cards at his disposal.

He began by immediately dispatching a delegation of the finest thinkers to call on the king, and among them he chose to include his son Cesare, to serve as interpreter. The young man, in fact, had studied French at the University of Pisa and spoke it perfectly. You'd think he'd taken his degree at the Sorbonne.

Already at the first meeting in Palazzo Venezia, where the king had taken up residence with all his officers, Cesare made the introductions. One by one, he presented the four dele-gates, speaking in French of course, and then translated to them the king's comments in a rapid-fire unadorned manner. He even ventured to crack a few jokes with the monarch, such as these, for example: "Have you noticed, Your Majesty, how much the people of Rome seem to like you? They seem to be real fans! I hope you're pleased! I even heard someone shout: 'Give this gentleman a place to stay in the Vatican! What are we waiting for? Let's make him pope immediately.' Your Majesty, if I were you, I'd give it some serious thought, there's never been a king who was made pope."

Charles of Valois burst out laughing loudly and com-mented: "You are very funny, and what's more, you speak my language with a truly enviable accent! Are you perchance one of my subjects?"

"No, Your Majesty, I only wish I was, but unfortunately I

was born in Rome. Ah, I almost forgot, I'm supposed to give you my father's warm regards!"

"And just who is your father?"

"The pope, your majesty, I am the son of Rodrigo Borgia, the current pontiff, Alexander VI."

"Why, by the Lord above! I had no idea that the pope could even have a son! He must have conceived you before beginning his career as a churchman!"

"No, sire, when I was born my father was already a cardinal. You understand, here it's considered a normal thing. I believe that there has never been a pope elected who didn't have children, a wife, and often concubines."

"Ha ha! You truly are an amusing miscreant! To speak in such terms of the holy clergy of the Roman Catholic apostolic church!"

In short, the meeting with the king of France was a huge success, especially for the young Borgia, who went back to his father and exclaimed: "Papa, this Charles VIII is a mouthful that you can chew up and swallow in the blink of an eye. I've set the table for you, with tablecloth and silverware. Now it's your turn."

The pope and the monarch met in the Vatican. When Charles of Valois entered the four-sided portico of the grand palace, the brass band of the papal militia struck up the expansive and majestic official march of the kingdom of France. Already this welcome made a certain impression on the young *guignol*, who lifted both arms and bowed before the pontiff who approached him all alone, followed at a short distance not by bishops, as one might have expected, but by a retinue of the most splendid ladies of the papal court.

From that moment onward, the cat and the mouse were engaged in a minuet.

Alexander VI addressed the young monarch in Latin:

Charles VIII

"*Excelsis rege qui degnastibus descendere hic Italiae magno honore civitas nostram exultes menomatus.*"

A look of terror appeared on Charles' face, and finally the pope burst out laughing: "Ha ha ha ha ha! I frightened you, didn't I, good sir? Don't be afraid, your majesty," he said in Italian, gesticulating as he spoke. "Since you got along so well with my son, I've appointed him, with your permission, to act as our interpreter."

"*Votre fils? Oh, je suis bien content de ça! Il est tellement aimable!*"

At that point Cesare walked in, a broad smile on his face, and, moving gracefully, made as if to kneel at the king's feet, but Charles lifted him up and embraced him. And here the hustling of the king began.

In the end, they came to an understanding: the pope gave the French army free passage through the Papal State; in exchange the French king agreed to leave the city of Rome immediately and promised the Borgias his protection and friendship. They stipulated that the pope's son Cesare would be attached to the French army, officially as the papal legate, but in reality as a truly privileged hostage.

Charles VIII soon reached Naples, where he was once again greeted as a conquering hero. Of course, King Alfonso II fled the capital of Southern Italy, took refuge in Sicily, and promptly abdicated; and so, without wasting any time, the king of France was able to appoint himself the legitimate ruler of Naples.

But it was at just this point that Spain and the other states of Italy and Europe began to feel uneasy at the excessive influence that the French seemed to be acquiring over the entire Italian peninsula. A decision was made to stop this threat before it could take shape. This meant the formation of the Holy League. To keep this project from being noticed, it was declared that the confederation aimed only to halt the advance of the Turks, but everyone knew that the most dangerous Turk around came from Paris and was named Charles, otherwise known as *le guignol*. This same Charles soon realized he was in danger of being trapped in in southern Italy by all these hostile forces. Therefore, consummate strategist that he was, he packed up puppets and marionettes and headed back north; in other words, he took to his heels.

The task that the pope had entrusted to his son-in-law, the thirty-year-old Giovanni Sforza, was that of leading the reconstituted Neapolitan army, reinforced by a papal contingent, to attack the French vanguard as it marched northward. But Giovanni took care to steer clear of any direct clashes between armies, which is to say he adopted the classical tactic pioneered by Fabius Maximus the "Cunctator." That Roman general followed the enemy troops from a safe distance and, having waited for his moment, moved in only when he sensed they were at a disadvantage. Brave Giovanni the latter-day delayer also followed from a distance, but unfortunately the French troops never found themselves at a disadvantage.

Meanwhile, Charles learned that the Venetian army was marching to intercept him, if possible before he and his troops crossed the Apennine Mountains. He therefore gave orders to step up the pace. When the French army reached Pisa it was given a jubilant welcome by the festive populace; beautiful women exclaimed at the sight of French soldiers and threw their arms around them, especially if they were on horseback. But the French monarch wished to waste no time, and he told his men: "We must make up our minds, either the joys of the flesh, or else we march afresh, which didn't so much need saying but I liked the rhyme." And with those words, he led his army northward into the Po Valley.

A king must know every so often when it is time to duck,
especially when passing under low gateways

As the French troops emerged from the Monti Carrarini the
artillery and the reserves were lagging behind. The French
headed down into the valley and slowed their pace, but at
Fornovo they clashed with the troops of the Holy League,
under the command of Francesco Gonzaga, marquess of
Mantua. The clash was brutal. Even though the French troops
were outnumbered, they managed to stave off a catastrophic
rout and avoid complete encirclement. They lost many men
but inflicted a comparable number of casualties on the army of
Italian allies. Disheartened but not beaten, the king passed
over the Alps and went back home to France.

In the end, at Amboise, where he had withdrawn to lick his
wounds, he had an accident truly befitting a clown. While riding a horse under a stone gate, like a complete *guignol*, he
smashed his head against the lintel, and was killed. The horse
was unhurt: it had wit enough to duck its head.

Alexander VI's son-in-law, hidden who knows where, was
likewise safe and sound. And so the pope flooded him with letters ordering him to turn over his command to other, more
competent generals and to come to speak with him immediately in Rome. The young Sforza, evidently overjoyed, arrived
in the capital of the Papal State and paid a call on his bride,
Lucrezia.

The Borgia pope at first gave no sign of open hostility
toward his miscreant son-in-law, and in fact on Palm Sunday,
we can observe the so-called lord of Pesaro at St. Peter's:
Giovanni sat among the high authorities of the church, right
next to Cesare, as he took the blessed palm frond that the pope
handed him during the paschal ritual. Back home, once
Giovanni had returned to the palazzo where Lucrezia now

lived, she told him that she was quite worried about her husband's immediate future. She told him that she wanted to try an old trick that was part of her family's stock-in-trade: specifically, a provocation that would allow them to discover what was really in store for her spouse.

After Giovanni left, while in the presence of the servants and the dishonest nurse, the pope's daughter burst into tears, wailing that she wouldn't put up with that husband of hers for another day, complaining that everyone thought of him as a weakling and a coward without dignity, both in battle and in everyday life. It was then that a serving girl, clearly hoping to comfort her, embraced her and whispered: "Never fear, my lady, in a just a few days you'll be rid of him."

And she retorted: "Rid of him? How do you mean? Is my husband going to be murdered, perchance?" And the dishonest nurse, eager to cut short that dangerous conversation, minimized: "What nonsense, murdered indeed! There are much easier and less violent ways of getting someone to abandon their gentle prey."

That was the end of that, and Adriana Mila issued an order: "All you women, back to work, and no gossiping!"

This was the signal for Lucrezia that her trap had functioned perfectly. When her husband returned home she went to him and warned him: "Things are not looking good, my dear. I know for certain that my brother Cesare and my father intend to get rid of you. The fact that they haven't yet threatened you openly means that they already have a plan to kill you or have you killed without witnesses: a far crueler solution."

And he replied: "Why, who told you that, your chambermaids?"

"Listen, my sweet Giovanni, from the tone of voice you're using I can see that my words haven't won you over, but at least take this piece of advice: stay at a safe distance for the next few days, and very close to the stables, with a steed already saddled and a bag full of provisions." With those words she kissed him and left, murmuring dolefully as she went: "I swear to you, I'd be ever so sad if they did you any harm."

But speak of the devil and out he comes. In fact, just then none other than Adriana, the woman who ran all the games, walked into the room and gaily announced: "Your brother is entering the palace right now."

"Oh, what a lovely surprise!" Lucrezia exclaimed in a well-acted tone of voice. With those words, she gestured to Giacomino, her most trusted servant, to put on an oversized cape, and when they reached the sculpture hall, she commanded the houseboy: "Quick, go hide behind that statue of Hercules and Cacus, stay still, and listen to everything that happens."

Lucrezia welcomed her brother with a broad smile and gave him a hug as she exclaimed in a loud voice: "What a magnificent surprise to see you like this, Cesare!"

Cesare kissed her tenderly and said, without a word of introduction: "Your father and I have decided that that husband of yours is no longer of any use to us, indeed if anything he is now more hindrance than help. I want you to prepare yourself to be a maiden once again, or even a widow."

Then he added, still speaking to his sister, who had been left speechless: "We shall speak of it soon, never fear; we will try to do everything in such a way that you will absolutely not be involved," and after a brief farewell the pope's son turned and left.

The first thing that Lucrezia did was to speak to Giacomino and tell him: "Did you hear every word of that? Go now and tell him."

Her servant went down to the stables and found Giovanni already mounted on his Turkish stallion.

He only had time to repeat Cesare's words: a quick kick of

his spurs and Lucrezia's husband was gone at a gallop, not even stopping at the troughs to let his horse get a drink of water.

The chronicles tell us that he arrived in the Marches just twenty-four hours later, a trip that would kill any horse. And in fact, when he reached the gates of Pesaro, his steed sprawled to the ground, dead.

Lucrezia has vanished. Run away, kidnapped? Who can say!

At that very moment, in Rome, Lucrezia went down into the stables, carrying a heavy bag, all alone, and ordered the stable boy to saddle her horse. Then she leapt into the saddle with the agility of an authentic amazon, placed her bag on the horse's back, spurred the animal, and set off at a brisk pace.

That very same evening Adriana noticed that Lucrezia was missing and, once she heard the vesper bells sounding, she became very worried. She sent a servant to inquire whether the girl might not have gone to stay with her mother, but she soon received word that Lucrezia hadn't been seen all day at Vannozza's.

All atremble the dishonest woman sent word to Lucrezia's father, who was dining with a few ambassadors, and in turn he immediately summoned the chief of the Vatican guards and ordered him to find out more. In the face of such an array of investigative forces, the truth soon came out: my lady Lucrezia had ridden out on horseback with bags and baggage, and was last seen heading toward the Appian Way. At first, they thought that she might have left the city, but the sentinels standing guard at every single gate were questioned, and there was no indication that she had left the city by any of those exits.

Another night went by before Pope Rodrigo was informed

that his youngest son Jofré had arrived from Naples the day before, and certainly met with his sister in her home.

The young man was tracked down in a tavern called the Locanda della Vacca, which everyone knew was Vannozza's property: several guards identified him and took him straight-away back to the Vatican. At first when questioned by his father, Jofré denied ever having met with Lucrezia, but when the pope bore down somewhat menacingly, he finally made up his mind to talk.

"Yes, father, I did see Lucrezia in her home. She was very upset, she said that she was positive that it was your intention, sir, and that of my brother Cesare, to kill her husband."

"What are you saying? How could she have come up with such a piece of arrant nonsense?"

"I don't know," the young man responded in a tense voice. "I didn't even wonder about it: I was too overwrought on my own account to have the presence of mind to delve into what was upsetting my sister."

"You were too overwrought? Why on earth?"

"Please, father. They say in Rome that Alexander VI is capable of reading the innermost thoughts of every subject of this city at the very instant in which they think them."

"What are you trying to imply?" blurted the pontiff. "What secrets are you talking about?"

"Well, for starters, the secret that concerns our family."

"Listen, don't play at the cabbala of riddles with me. Speak clearly."

"I'm referring to what happened to me, and what happened when my brother Cesare decided to have some fun and take my wife to bed, his own brother's wife!"

"But what are you saying?"

"That's enough, father, now you're the one who's playing at the cabbala of false innocence with me. Farewell, I'm going back to Naples."

Jofré Borgia

"Stop right there!" The pope grabbed him by the arm and pulled him close. "It's true, Cesare ravished your wife: it's a horrible thing. I learned of it just this morning, and I gave him a brutal dressing-down. Then Cesare turned on me, shouting: 'Even if you are the pope, that doesn't give you the right to stick your nose into my business. Why don't you worry about your own amorous liaisons? I've never come to preach morality to you, and if I did I'd have recriminations that could go on for days.'"

And so the Holy Father learned that Lucrezia was well aware of Cesare's amorous misdeeds, and when she was finished with those revelations she burst out in a fit of shrieks, insults, and even blasphemy toward one and all, against her brother and even against the pope himself.

Continuing with his account, Jofré recalled: "'Enough is enough!' Lucrezia screamed in horror. 'At this point, I need to be out of this situation, I'd rather simply disappear than go on living in this swamp of a rotten life. It's unseemly! On a single day, I have discovered that my nearest and dearest are plotting to murder my husband and that my brother Cesare is lusting after our younger brother's bride. And for no good reason, just idle pleasure!' And as she went on screaming," Jofré continued, "Lucrezia started throwing open the various chests and pulling out clothing and linen, stuffing it into a bag, as she exclaimed: 'Far better to be buried alive in a convent than to go on living in a world of such infamy!'"

"That's it!" Rodrigo snapped. "That's it! She's hiding in a convent! How could I have failed to think of it before this?"

And finally the pope, after ordering his inquisitors to search all the convents of the city with a fine-toothed comb, was able to discover the holy place where his daughter had taken refuge.

It was the convent of the Sisters of Saint Sixtus.

Rodrigo immediately hurried to that convent, without retinue or entourage: obviously, what was upsetting him was the thought that some caprice of his daughter's might unravel all his well-laid plans.

Above all, though, he was filled with sincere love for her: "I really do love you! I don't know what I wouldn't do for you."

"Father, a love like the one you're offering is of no interest to me," she answered him, "it's only half a love. Do you think that the existence to which you've condemned me is a fitting one? First you make me spend my entire childhood convinced that the remarkably uninteresting man who was sleeping with my mother was my actual father. If nothing else, he seemed to love me. At the same time, you let me and my siblings believe that you were a kindly cardinal, a man of the cloth, and a very powerful one. And, just as bright as the morning sun, one day you tell us who you really are. Hardly a generous friend of the household but my mother's lover for the past twenty years, during which time you had the pleasure of getting her pregnant not once but four times. And finally, we discover that you are the most powerful cardinal in Rome, soon to become pope, a ladykiller who goes about insatiably collecting amorous conquests. And in fact, you fall in love with a beautiful friend of mine, little more than a girl, and you decide to take her as your lover. As a matter of sheer convenience, you marry her off to the son of my nurse, a poor miserable wretch with no particular skills or talents, and only one eye, to boot. Then it's my turn. So you decide with the assistance of my brother Cesare, your worthy son, that I may come in handy to you as a way to rope in the duke of Milan as part of your schemes, because he normally keeps you from doing exactly as you please. So you choose one of his nephews, he too an illegitimate son, and as it happens the lord of Pesaro, another Sforza, and you gift wrap him for me as a husband, without so much as consulting me, after introducing me to him (remember clearly, I was thirteen years old at the time), as if I would be interested in a man twice my age. You behaved more considerately when you took me to the papal stables and showed me a purebred colt and added: 'This is the finest of the hundred horses that belong to the pope. Try this one first, and if you don't like it and you see another one that suits you better, make a different choice, put a halter on the horse you like best, have it properly groomed, and take it home.' But to come back to the other colt, young Giovanni Sforza, you told me to take that one home too. I made do with what you gave me, he was hardly the man of my dreams, but first of all he was in love with me, and second I discovered with him for the first time what it means to be thought of as a human being and not just a pawn to be moved across the chessboard of your interests and ambitions."

The pope, after a long silence, spoke to his daughter in a subdued voice: "I have to confess, you seem to know me better than I know myself. So I won't waste your time and mine by using rhetoric and a show of emotion to defend what I have done here, how I have led my life and how I continue to do so. But I swear to you that I will do everything I can to get out of this labyrinth in which I find myself wandering, lost, and often—please believe me—so bereft of hope that I've thought more than once of giving up everything."

"Don't say that, father. When you say 'giving up everything up' are you talking about abdicating, or even better, resigning and retiring to live in a monastery yourself? Father, I'm sorry I'm not in the mood right now to burst into a series of loud guffaws."

"All right, I understand. It's not a good day for me, but I just hope that you've chosen to remain within these walls to meditate and do your best to understand and forgive the madness that has taken us and dragged us all out of our minds and our piety, even for ourselves."

And so, with a stage exit worthy of a *hypocrites* of Greek theater, the pope stalked off, displaying tears streaming down his face.

And at this point we'll have to come up with a new skit.
As long as it's not clownish

Now Alexander VI was more relaxed. He felt certain that
Lucrezia would not be able to take the strictures of her monas-
tic vacation for much longer, and that she would emerge from
it with a new spirit of resignation. But before a few more days
had passed, the news that the pope's daughter had forever
abandoned her sumptuous and sophisticated home and chosen
to cloister herself in a convent began to spread throughout the
populace with an irrepressible clamor. It was obvious by now
that the entire plot of physically eliminating her spouse, so long
and lovingly nurtured, was no longer practicable. He'd have to
come up with a new plot, a new skit, less drastic and above all
more acceptable, at the risk of reducing everything to a farce.

The next day Cesare grabbed the knocker on the convent's
portal door and pounded loudly. A small hatch opened in the
wooden door and the face of a conversa appeared. She asked:
"Who are you looking for?"

And Cesare replied: "I am Cardinal Borgia, the brother of
my lady Lucrezia, please open the door."

"I'm sorry, Your Eminence, but I have orders that no one,
not even close family members, can enter the cells of our
guests."

The conversa tried to close the little panel but Borgia's hand
shot through, grabbing the veil of the young religious, and
forcing her to thrust her entire face into the little postern. A
moment later, the door swung open and the unwelcome visitor
had grabbed the young woman by her hair, forcing her to walk
on tiptoe, and ordered her to lead him to his sister's bedroom.
They crossed the four-sided portico and climbed a steep
staircase, at the top of which was a two-paneled door.

"Open up!" ordered the cardinal with his usual arrogance.

A bolt was shot back, and from behind the door that swung

open appeared Lucrezia. When she saw her brother, the young woman turned pale then and there and was unable to get out a single word. Cesare kicked the door shut with the heel of his boot. Then he threw his arms around his sister's shoulders, pulled her to him, and burst into tears, murmuring: "I love you. I was terrified at the thought that you might do something reckless on my account."

"You, terrified? For me? Perhaps because you finally realized that you are the playwright orchestrating this whole farce?"

"Don't you start too, by God! Everyone has been kicking me as if I were a mangy dog! Our father insulted me and called me a bloody cutthroat and a whoremonger, on account of my little dalliance with our brother's wife. And when I told him that it hadn't been my idea and that she had taken the initiative, lusty as she lunged at me already bare naked, he hit me in the face with such a mighty punch that he knocked me to the ground. Now our brother, Jofré, after his sweet little wife lyingly told him that I'd taken her by force, has ordered two of his henchmen to find me and kill me on the spot, from what I hear."

"Don't tell me, the terrible mastiff falls prey to the silly hen."

The grotesque is the most effective medium through which to attain wisdom

"Do you know what and where I feel like I am right now?"
"Tell me, where?"
"A few months ago, to celebrate the fourth anniversary of our marriage, I had decided with Giovanni, my husband, whom you call a runagate and a miscreant, to leave Pesaro and travel to Ferrara, where we knew that a great fair was being held in honor of Duke Ercole d'Este. And so, after we got to

that city, we chanced to attend an evening's entertainment that was unbelievable, with its spectacular fantasy and rich array of theatrical contrivances. We were first of all greatly astonished to discover that the actors were speaking, not in Latin or incomprehensible dialects as they usually did, but in the vernacular, the ordinary spoken Italian vernacular of the people of Ferrara, a clean and elegant language. But the strange thing is that, in contrast, the poses and movements of the characters were not human but entirely animalike, and the actors in particular were behaving like dogs. They wagged their tails (the tail was moved by wires that the actor himself could pull), they sniffed each other's behinds every time they met, they snarled to greet one another, they licked each other's noses and necks, the males lifted their legs when they wanted to urinate and, every so often, they put on a display of animal courtship with moaning, rubbing, and to finish up in glory, a full-fledged canine mounting, with the female bent over and the male covering her from above. All of it in the most nonchalant manner imaginable, on the sidewalks of the streets. Nothing surprising about it, in a way: after all animals have no sense of shame. Each individual wore a mask that alluded to a different breed of dog. There were mastiffs, hunting dogs, and ordinary pets, while the chorus was made up of mutts. To emphasize these differences, the actors who led the pack wore fine leather collars with golden studs around their necks, while the mutts were forced to settle for rope collars and rusty chains."

Finally Cesare interrupted: "Excuse me but why are you telling me the story of this whole piece of theater? What allegory are you talking about?"

"Why, my dear brother, the reference is to us: we're the stars of the show. In fact, the title of that strange play was *The City of Dogs*, and I later learned that like nearly everything that we write here in Italy, it has been translated into English. A theatrical troupe tried to put on a production of it in London, under a different title and with appropriate modifications, but King Henry VII put a halt to that and I hear that he sent the whole troupe to jail, including the prompter."

"Very good, I see that our cities and their princes are becoming famous all around the world," her brother replied, "if for no reason other than orgies, scandals, and obscenities."

"Ah, but there's a detail I neglected to mention," said Lucrezia. "In the production we saw, there were children on the proscenium, and at the height of the most tasteless of the grotesque pantomimes, they could do nothing more than look on in horror. Then they pulled the broad piece of cloth that served as a curtain across the stage, as if to erase that obscene and cruel world that the actors had portrayed up to that point. Immediately a song could be heard, like something out of a fairy tale, and the children began to dance and hug each other with gestures of surpassing fondness and purity in their tenderness. And that was when images of the two of us—you and me—appeared before my eyes, back when we were just small, when we all lived in the same home, and when we played house together."

"Yes! I remember that game. Each of us played a different part, Juan and I took turns being the father, you, Lucrezia, were the mother, and little Jofré was our son, and in that game we really did all love each other."

"I remember how I would always say: 'When I grow up I want to marry my brother and live with him.' "

"That's right, and I was jealous of Juan, who was two years older than me, and always acted as if he was the favorite. I always had to be the bishop uncle, our family friend."

"Certainly, but you have to admit that every so often I preferred you, and I demanded you as my husband."

"And then we'd go and lie down together in the bed as if we really were married. I never forgot how we caressed each other."

"But I often wonder," Lucrezia said, "why we felt such an urgent need to pretend we were a family?"

And Cesare shot back: "No doubt because we instinctively felt that what we took for our family really wasn't—that it was a fiction, and so we dreamt up another story, even though it was every bit as false."

"Speaking of imaginary love affairs and other unseemly topics, I've heard that it is whispered all over Rome, about the two of us, that we are supposedly incestuous lovers."

"Yes, I've heard this infamous slander myself, and that is why it strikes me as best that we stay as far from each other as we can, lest we give the tongue-waggers more of a chance to sully our reputations."

"I understand. You're saying I should leave?"

"Yes, that would certainly be best."

"May I at least give you one last embrace?"

"Certainly, and go with God."

In Rome everything that is discarded eventually winds up bobbing in the river

Two days later, early in the morning, ferrymen working on the Tiber spotted a body bobbing in the stream. The drowned man was dressed in sumptuous garments, made of fine cloth picked out in glittering gold thread. They soon learned that this was no less a personage than the firstborn son of the pontiff Alexander VI, namely Juan Borgia. His body bore multiple stab wounds. Who could have murdered and scornfully dumped into the river such a powerful individual, a man with a career ahead of him that promised a triumphant series of successes?

All through Rome there were diatribes implicating first this, then that rival as the murderer. Of course, famous families were mentioned, the Orsinis and the Colonnas and others of their ilk. But in the end suspicions narrowed to the murdered man's own family, and the name that was uttered in every tavern and even in the most august palazzi of highborn Rome was that of Cesare Borgia, Juan's brother.

Among all the residents of that city, the one who was most distraught, on the verge of utter despair, was certainly Juan's father, Pope Alexander VI. The entire populace wondered, however, why the very monarch of Rome failed to order the police to carry out a ruthless and thorough investigation. In fact, without even answering those who asked him whether he had any idea as to possible motives for this killing and who might have done it, the victim's father remained silent and impassive. The logical conclusion was worthy of a well wrought Pasquinade: in fact, many of the subjects of the holy realm repeated a single phrase: "The pope says nothing because he knows that the murderer felt right at home—in his *own* home!"

And so Pope Alexander VI was automatically transformed into the chief suspect of that crime. At that point, everyone felt sure that he had fallen under the sway of his own terrible but favorite son.

Let cowards not seek liberty by asking it of those who hold power!

The terrible son wasn't too worried about that accusation. He had a program to complete, and he had come to an agreement with his father: he intended to persuade Giovanni Sforza, who was still Lucrezia's husband, to renounce her in order to preserve his power over the city of Pesaro.

In order to achieve that objective he would have to speak roughly and harshly to that cowardly husband of his sister's.

With that aim in mind he went down to the Marches with only a skeleton guard to escort him.

And there he tracked down Giovanni who, turning pale at his words, was forced to hear out young Borgia's proposal: "My good friend," he said, "here's the way matters stand. We offer you two alternatives: the first is that you agree to sign a document in which you declare yourself to be impotent and therefore incapable of having carnal knowledge of any woman. The second is that you acknowledge in a judge's presence that you have of your own free will decided not to have any sexual congress with Lucrezia."

"Why, indeed," retorted Giovanni in an impetus of dignity and courage, "you are asking me to tell a lie that would besmirch my bride as well as me! How can anyone believe that any man, however foolish and weak, as you are hoping I will allow myself to be perceived, could remain indifferent, shorn of all and any carnal desire in the presence of a woman as splendid as your sister?"

"All right," the ruthless Cesare reassured him, "if you don't feel up to admitting your own impotence, you're free to do as you will, I respect the worth of any man's expectations of dignity. I only hope that luck is on your side. My brother, this is a world full of traps and perils, you might happen to run into a wild bull that has escaped its corral and in its mad fury might trample anyone underfoot, or you might meet with a religious fanatic who takes you for a heretic, chains you to a pole, and burns you alive. Or you might happen to gulp down a glass of wonderful wine meant for someone else that just happens to contain a tremendous poison, and end your days amidst terrible convulsions and inhuman screams. These are things that happen! In any case, think it over carefully, we'll talk again before long. Ah, I almost forgot, if you wish to talk it over with your wife, that is to say, my sister, you should know that since yesterday she is no longer in the convent of St. Sixtus where she first took refuge."

Juan Borgia

Cesare Borgia,
"the terrible son"

"I suppose you tore her away from that refuge yourself?" the young man asked angrily.

"No, she left of her own free will, she's vanished, and search for her though we might, we haven't found a sign of her. If you happen to see her, please be so good as to let us know. After all, we're her family!"

"Ha ha ha! That's a rich one!"

Let us leave Cesare for a moment and move into the countryside around Ferrara. On the banks of the so-called Second Po, a branch of the river running down to the sea, we will find an ancient convent that was abandoned by the nuns in the fourteenth century because they were afraid they might be struck down by the raging plague of that year. A group of religious had taken over the ruins a few months ago and were now rebuilding it.

A young man on horseback drew up outside the front gate and asked something of a bricklayer. The mason showed him the way, leading him inside, into a four-sided portico. The young man dismounted and almost immediately a fairly corpulent woman strode up to him, shoving him back.

"Get out of here! Who are you looking for?"

Immediately Lucrezia's voice rang out: she was leaning out a window and shouting: "Leave him alone! That's my husband!" And then: "Giovanni, I'll be right down!"

A moment later, Lucrezia emerged into the courtyard: "Oh, Giovanni, what a pleasure to see you at last!"

Giovanni replied: "What were you thinking, to come hide here of all places? Unless I'm mistaken this is an old monastery, it should be child's play for your father to find you here."

"No. It was a monastery once, but now it's a community of Pizzocchere!"

"Pizzocchere? What on earth are those?"

"They're sisters minor, who need no special permission to

form an order. That means no one in the official clergy could possibly track us down here."

"It's lucky that Giacomino, our faithful servant, managed to catch me just in time, I was about to gallop out of the stables when he caught up with me . . . I don't even know where I was going, but as far away as possible."

"So what's happened?"

"Your brother Cesare came to see me, sent by your father; with the aim of having our marriage annulled he demanded that I sign a document declaring myself impotent!"

"Impotent? And did you sign it?"

"Not yet, but I can't see how I can avoid having to."

"Why, he's a shameless dog!"

"That's right, and at the same time he made it very clear to me that if I refuse to accept this solution of theirs I might suddenly have an accident of some kind, or I could simply be eliminated, by some mysterious stranger. By the way, I have to give you some news that will cause you great sorrow . . . "

"Oh God, something else? What now?"

"Your brother Juan . . . He's been found murdered."

"I was already aware of that."

"Ah, you were? But do you know that everyone in Rome is convinced that the murderer was none other than your brother Cesare?"

"Yes, I know that too. I also know that our father is considered to be guilty in his turn, inasmuch as he certainly knew who did it but asked forgiveness for the murderers."

"That's right, and in that way he has revealed his own connivance in the matter."

"Sadly, that's the way it is. And I also know that afterward he went into a terrible crisis; for three days on end no one saw hide nor hair of him, he locked himself up in his room and they heard him wail in desperation and sob and weep all day and all night. And where was his son, the murderer? Perhaps at his father's side? No! He had hurried down to Pesaro to see you and threaten you with death if you failed to comply with his will. And that is why I fled from the convent in Rome, I never want to see any member of my family again, I can't stand to go on living with this terrible curse that they have laid on my head, that is, the name of Borgia."

"And now, in order to ensure that you can live without fear or violence, I'm going to be forced to renounce all claims to you. And to think that with you I've lived the happiest years of my life."

"Don't worry about me, just worry about saving your own life. You know what I think? There's a solution!"

"What is it?"

"Your uncle, Ludovico the Moor, is a Sforza just like you; he owes you some consideration, because after all it was at his behest that you agreed to take me as a wife, and it served his purposes too. Isn't that true?"

"Certainly, it's true, but it won't do any good."

"Why not? Come on, have the courage to try."

"I've already done it, my sweet Lucrezia, and it did me no good at all; in fact, if anything, I came away mortified more than ever."

"Explain why you were mortified."

"I asked him to intervene, to protect us from the brutality of the Borgias, and he, Ludovico the Moor, suggested the following. He said: 'You know what you need to do? You need to prove to one and all that not only are you not impotent but that you are a real stallion.' 'And how can I do that?' 'Well, you present yourself before a qualified jury composed of all men, including of course the papal legate, several representatives of the leading guilds, and even a few women, and especially a couple of pimps, so that they can personally verify your prowess. And then, bare naked, you will undertake the great challenge: ready, set, go-o-o-o! That is when a fine woman strides onto the stage with sumptuous breasts and buttocks, she too all naked and lusty, inviting you to duel with her. And you, like any self-respecting ram, immediately display your attributes in a splendid erection, and you take her, once, twice, three times . . . oh, well, let's just say twice, that's already plenty . . . ' "

Lucrezia stared at him, appalled, and exclaimed: "Incredible . . . is that really what he said to you? With those words? It's certainly true that even the most heartbreaking tragedies are always at risk of turning into obscene farces. By the way, I've forgotten even to ask if you've had something to eat."

"Don't worry, I'll find an inn along the way."

"What an idea! Night is falling and it makes no sense for you to be out on the open road in the dark. Listen to me: spend the night here, and you can leave again tomorrow morning at sunrise."

"Sleep here? Is there a room for me?"

"Yes, my room."

"Are you sure of what you're saying?"

"Listen, I don't know what will happen after this. This could very well be the last time I see you. I want to give you—and take for myself—a fond memory of our time together."

In the morning, Giovanni mounted his horse and rode off to Milan where, in the presence of Ludovico the Moor, Cardinal Ascanio Sforza, and Cesare Borgia, he prepared to sign a declaration of his own impotence: "I am complying with your demands, but you," he said to Lucrezia's brother, "must at the same time promise me that you will finally leave your sister in peace! That is, that you will let her live her life as she sees fit."

At the same time, Lucrezia, who had gone to Rome for the occasion, was signing a document before the pope and two notaries in which she declared that her marriage with Giovanni Sforza had never been consummated. Her father bid her farewell with a hug: "Never fear, I have given orders that you are not to be bothered anymore. I want you to be completely free and, if possible, happy. Listen to me, I want you to stay for just a few more hours. I need you to attend a meeting that I'm going to have with all the bishops and cardinals."

"Why?"

"It's going to be a surprise, my dear. I'm certain that you'll be astonished at what I'm going to say, almost as astonished as the assembled curia."

"But how can I sit among the clergy? I'm a woman!"

"Come into this room. This is where the nuns who assist me keep their outfits; I'm sure you'll find one your size. When I see you in the hall, I'll start delivering my speech."

The holy about-face

Shortly thereafter the consistory began in the Gallery of Tapestries. Alexander, seated on his throne, rose to his feet and started speaking in a flat voice, with apparent difficulty: "Allow me to inform you of my state of mind in the aftermath of my eldest son's murder. No greater grief could have struck me, I felt an exorbitant love for my son, the way any father would for a sweet and lovely boy like Juan. In the face of the blow I've been dealt, I can no longer make a wholehearted commitment to the papacy or any other important duty."

A slight buzz resounded in the gallery, and the pontiff looked around, as if trying to puzzle out its meaning, and then went on: "If my office allowed me to manage seven papacies, I'd give them all up to get this son of mine back, safe and sound. Certainly, this punishment has swept my life into chaos and confusion not because *he* deserved it, but surely for some sin of *mine*, first and foremost for having thought of the advantages I could take from this office, forgetting that I was elected not to leave things as I found them, but to modify them in their entirety. Well, if this harsh message goes unheard, the only foreseeable consequence is that I and the church as a whole will once again be admonished and even more harshly punished. The custom of alienating ecclesiastical goods has endured till now: that is to say, selling church property, trading in it, profiting from that trade. And let me be clear, that profit has never devolved to evangelical charity; instead it has always dissolved into the rivulets of power that you all know far too well.

"From this day forward the perpetration of this unworthy activity is completely forbidden. And while we're at it, let me make it clear that we're talking about banks. I've carefully reread all the words of the Holy Gospels and, just think, I never found even the slightest reference to the idea that, in order for the church to grow and be valued by the poor and the wretched, it might be necessary to found an earthly palace within which, through loans and commercial transactions involving trade and business, assets and treasures are piled up for a revolutionary emancipation of mankind. I've never found even the slightest reference to such a thing!

"On the other hand, in rereading my Bible, I found the story of a prophet who laid out in all directions, clubbing the merchants who were doing business in the temple, because the priests had decided to allow the moneylenders and profiteers to set up their stalls there.

"Just to be clear, there is a rule that you must accept, namely that from now on no cardinal is allowed to hold more than one episcopal see and no cardinal can receive from his prebends an annual income of more than six thousand ducats. Simony, which is something I myself have practiced, will be punished from this day forth with anathema, that is to say, excommunication. Yes, let me say it again, I want first and foremost to prevent anyone calling me a pointless jabberer who simultaneously levels a finger to accuse his brethren of ignominious deeds while with the other hand pocketing cash and benefits, perpends and offices, for himself and for his children and relations. The only way to save this church and to find renewal so that we can present ourselves to the faithful, transformed into new men, is to press the pedal of the lathe in such a way as to forge new consciences and renewed charity.

"And so I ask you: how can we, who claim to be intermediaries of God, charged with bringing justice to the last and the least, receive salaries that rise to as much as a hundred times what our servants are paid, starting with the lowliest parish priests? Do you remember the story of the son of the rich glutton who asked Jesus: 'Master, what must I do to be worthy of walking at Your side toward the kingdom of Our Lord?' And do you remember what his Master told him? Well, just imagine that in the present day the same young man were to ask the Messiah the same question. Now what would the Son of God reply to him? Would He say nothing more than: 'Put off your riches'? No. He would add: 'Free yourself of all the privileges that attach to your station in life, the prebends, bequests, and contracts, and all profits of corruption, to say nothing of the depredations that everyone in your gang carries out, without fear of indictment and punishment.' And here we should have the courage to denounce the curia first and foremost—a curia that is sunk up to its neck in a morass of corruption and extortion. The laymen of every province find themselves shaken down and oppressed by the ecclesiastical administrators, and if they try to rebel they inexorably become the victims of yet another robbery.

"And in conclusion (I know that with this request of mine I risk tossing a huge boulder into a pond full of frogs), I also ask that an end be put once and for all to the practice of concubines being collected for bishops, cardinals, and priests, starting with the pope himself."

All the participants in the consistory, upset and over-whelmed, and convinced that the speech was over, rose to their feet. One and all, deeply concerned, they began discussing the Holy Father's proposals with their neighbors.

"Be still, all of you, I'm not done," Alexander VI silenced the room. They all turned to look at him and sank back into their chairs. "I wanted to warn you that for the past three days I have been meeting for hours at a time with ten cardinals from the reform council, and that together we have been drafting a working platform. Don't believe for a moment that we intend nothing more than to tickle the consciences of the church a lit-tle, in order to break up the monotonous rhythm of the cogs and flywheels of power. We shall impose this transformation so that all the rot that has stuck to our boots is cleaned off, be it at the cost of walking barefoot from now on."

As the room emptied of those who had been summoned, the pope remained alone, sorting through the papers of his speech. Suddenly he was literally seized by a pair of arms, forc-ing him to scatter his papers in all directions, and a face glued itself to his, showering it with kisses. Naturally, all this affec-tion was being lavished upon him by none other than his daughter Lucrezia.

"That was just wonderful, father," she exclaimed with tears running down her face, uttering cries of joy. "The things that you said! The courage of your words! I'm still wondering whether your emotional turmoil really did produce the meta-morphosis that you have bestowed upon us! Until an hour ago, I truly hated you, my father, for everything you've always rep-resented. But now I feel a love for you that is unlike anything I've ever experienced. I beg you, continue relentlessly in this task you have decided to take on, don't betray the faith of thousands of people who, like me, are waiting for the miracle of a truly holy church."

Lucrezia immediately sent a missive to the Pizzocchere sisters who had given her a place to stay in Ferrara, and it read more or less as follows: "God is truly great and unpredictable. He has transformed my father from a tyrant into a Christian full of humanity. For now I am going to stay in Rome. I wish to experience this extraordinary development from up close."

One Florentine delegate who was in the Eternal City commented, incredulously: "The reform council sits every morning in the papal palace."[2] Another chronicler observed that "everyone works with such zeal and alacrity that, watching all those busy bishops and cardinals, you wonder at every turn whether you are in the Vatican or in some ballad recounting the most flagrantly absurd tale imaginable."

Those who have decided to redeem themselves from sin should be ready to climb up onto the executioner's pulpit

A few days later the pontiff's son, Cesare, came to see him and asked to speak urgently out of the presence of his bishops. They secluded themselves in a large room where workers were repairing the walls. Cesare gestured to the workers to exit the room and then prepared to attack his father who was sitting calmly on a bench.

"Father, you put on a truly stirring skit, my compliments!"

"I knew that you would have a hard time accepting this decision of mine, son," the pope said, beating him to the punch. "Haven't you ever had a crisis of conscience over anything? For instance, are you always comfortable with the kind of life you're leading?"

"Father, if I were you, I'd stop talking about me and I'd lend an ear, as the phrase goes, to what's being said about you

[2] *Ibid.*, p. 129.

by all those pretending right now to be your supporters but who, like you, seem as if they'd all just tumbled off their mounts, blinded on the road to Damascus, repentant and ready to transform the world."

"I know," the pontiff interrupted him, "that many of them are willing to play along merely in the hope that I'll stumble and can be eliminated. Outside of this place, though, there are thousands of men and women who believe in what I have vowed to accomplish. It is on their behalf that I have gone mad, as you all believe."

"It's such an odd thing. You've written letters to Savonarola in which you're openly contemptuous, do you remember? You even threatened him, telling him you were ready to intervene with armed force against him and the mass of Piagnoni who support him."

"Yes, but I've always respected him, and even now I continue to think of him as a fanatic but still a person of great human value."

"I know. You've even invited him to come and visit so that the two of you can come up with a very different way to run the church. And that's not all! I've also read your proposals for the consistory: you borrowed his words to better illustrate your proposals, and I've actually memorized those words: 'We speak nothing but truths, but it is your sins that prophesy against you. We want to lead men toward a more honest way of life. And you instead want to go on guiding them into lust, pomp, and pride, since you've ravaged the world and corrupted its people by dragging them into swindles and lies.'"

"Yes, it's true, I used his words. But I did so because I'm convinced that they were authentic and efficacious, words that can shift the conscience down to its very foundation."

"Good work, my father, but do you know what all this incitement of the simple folk will lead to?"

"Yes, to my throne being overturned, unless I'm capable of holding fast to it with all my might."

"No, it will lead you straight to martyrdom. And is that truly what you desire? Do you want a scaffold with a hangman's rope and noose all ready for you and a fire that burns even brighter because of the gunpowder they've tossed in the flames to make them roar and seethe? I wish that, instead of being here in Rome, in a year's time we could be together in Florence and we could look out the windows of the Palazzo della Signoria to behold the conclusion of the great adventure of your holy man, Savonarola. You must know by now that the ruling council of Florence has already deprived him of their protection and his trial is expected to conclude with a death sentence."

"Yes, and I also know that a few months ago you tried your hardest to eliminate the holy brother with all his followers."

"Whatever are you saying, father? Just what am I supposed to have done?"

"Oh, nothing, merely that you arranged a counterfeit document to persuade the bishop of Perugia to issue an order that I supposedly sent from Rome concerning Savonarola. An order of excommunication, naturally. Counterfeit, of course, but taken for authentic even by the Medicis' signoria council, at least at first. Luckily everyone then discovered that it was an egregious fake, my dear Cesare, and you know exactly what I'm talking about."

"And are you saying that I arranged the 'fake' in question?"

"Yes, my dear boy, and you did it behind my back. I can always spot your falsehoods, even from a mile away."

"Ah, now I see, it didn't do a bit of good, I should have known. The only reason I came here at all was to put you on alert. I assure you that once you get a clear picture of what's going on and you're running for your life from a lynch mob, I'll be there to come to your aid. I kiss you, father, *adiós*."

Private parties in ecclesiastical circles, it was well known, had been recently prohibited by Alexander VI's new reforms. But parties that did not entail secrecy in any programmatic way, that is, parties where everything that took place was open and aboveboard, pure and chaste, including the dancing and the songs, were allowed and looked upon favorably by one and all. Especially when they were held under the auspices of orders such as the Humiliati, as was this one. The Humiliati had finally been freed from the threat of unappealable suppression by the Holy Father in person. The party was being held precisely in order to cheerfully say good riddance to the narrowly averted peril.

A truly unpredictable amorous event

On this occasion we find Lucrezia as the guest of honor: she had also been selected by the master of the assembled group as hostess. She therefore had the task of welcoming the guests and setting them at their ease, introducing them to each other. Working with her and lending a hand was Giulia Farnese, whom Lucrezia attempted to involve in the party, since the poor girl was beside herself and from time to time simply burst into tears, complaining that for the past few weeks the pontiff had completely abandoned her.

A group of musicians welcomed every new guest. The atmosphere was practically that of a peasant *mariazzo*, or wedding party, where courting duels were normally held between young men and maidens. Everyone did their best to display cheerfulness and giddy glee. Suddenly, a crowd of young Neapolitans made their way into the party, instantly producing a wave of euphoria among the milling guests with the sudden charge of good natured affability they brought with them. Among them was a particularly youthful lad, perhaps eighteen years of age, who introduced himself to Lucrezia with an exaggerated courtly bow, one which however won him a heartfelt burst of laughter. As he regained his standing position, he overbalanced and fell to the ground. Lucrezia hastened to help him to his feet and unexpectedly found herself locked in the young man's arms. They stayed in that position for a long time, gazes locked as if under some enchantment.

No doubt about it, this was a classic case of love striking like a lightning bolt. And indeed for the rest of the evening the two were never once apart. They told each other everything about themselves, in a conversation that could perfectly well have fit into a production of Romeo and Juliet.

"Who are you?" the young man asked.

And she replied: "I am a lady in waiting."

"To whom?"

"To Donna Lucrezia! Do you know her?"

"No, but I've heard lots of things about her . . . "

"Good things or bad things?"

"I'd say magnificent things. In Naples, where I live, the pope's daughter has practically become a legend for lovers."

"I'm sure she'd be flattered to hear these sentiments. Unfortunately she's not here today, no one seems to know where she's gotten to. But what about you? Who are you?"

"I'm just a groom in the stables of the Duke of Naples. And he's not here either."

"Oh look, they're handing out papier-mâché masks, do you want one?"

"Well . . . if you're so keen on being spared the sight of my face . . . "

"Don't be silly. Soon everyone will be wearing a mask, and we can't be the only ones not playing by the rules of the game."

As they were slipping on their masks, Lucrezia asked: "But tell me, what is your name?"

"I'd rather keep that to myself, because if I'm recognized

Alfonso of Aragon

here there's a good chance I'll be tossed bodily out the back door."

"But why?"

"My family is hated by the Colonnas, and this is after all their home."

"Fine, I'll give you a name of my own choice. How about Alfonso? That's a self-important name, do you like it?"

"Sure, it's good enough. And what is your name?"

"That doesn't matter: why don't you go ahead and think of a name for me, too?"

"Fine, I'll call you Emiliana."

"Ah, good name, I like it!"

"But why did you want me to invent one for you?"

"Because I'm here too under a false pretext."

"A false pretext, you say? What do you mean by that?"

"I'm a conversa, a servant nun, and I ran away from my convent on the very day I was supposed to take my vows."

"Ah, that's serious! And you think I should believe you?"

"If you prefer, I could tell you that I'm a courtesan and I'm here to make my living."

We promptly come to the moment when Lucrezia and Alfonso find themselves completely alone in a suite in an aristocratic palazzo.

"What just happened?" asked the young man. "Just a moment ago we were here, with Giulia, that crybaby, and with her was that other woman you called nurse, and also my old friend Ludovico. Then I went over to the window for a moment to get a breath of fresh air, and when I came back everyone was gone. I went looking for you and I found all the rooms empty and now I've finally found you here, all alone. Where did everyone else go?"

"They all left."

"But why?"

"They said it was because an accident befell the son of Adriana, the nurse, who is also the husband of Giulia Farnese."

"Oh, I'm sorry to hear that! What happened to him?"

"Don't worry, it's nothing serious."

"And they took my old friend with them when they went . . . Why?"

"Because I don't believe that the story of the accident is true, they just invented it so that the two of us could be alone, what a thoughtful gift, don't you think? Or don't you like it?"

"No, no, quite the opposite! I like it! And whose house is this?"

"Mine, I live here with the nurse . . . "

"Your house? Of all things! Forgive me, but I'm worried about my old friend . . . Do you think they'll come back? And when?"

"Don't you worry about them. Why don't you make yourself comfortable, instead?" and she pointed him to a sofa.

He sat down, looked around, and then asked again: "Forgive me if I behave like a stunned loony bird, but it's just that . . . You make me feel quite shy . . . "

"Shy? Why on earth would I make you feel shy?"

"I can't really say, but the minute I laid eyes on you I said to myself: 'This isn't any ordinary girl, this is a queen.'"

"Oh, thank you! You're really too kind!" She took his hand and asked: "Forgive me for asking, but are you really twenty years old?"

"Well, I confess that I told you a story earlier . . . The truth is that I'm seventeen, or I'm going to be soon . . . "

"Well, don't worry, I'm only one year older than that."

"One year older than what? Seventeen or twenty?"

"One year older than seventeen."

"Ah, that's good . . . "

"And do you have a girlfriend in Naples?"

"Yes, but we never see each other, in part because she doesn't really know . . . "

"Are you saying that you've never . . . how to put this . . . declared your feelings?"

"That's right . . . you know, I may act pretty self-confident but . . . I feel like I can tell you, I've never been with a woman . . . "

"Really?"

"No, truth be told, I'm actually not entirely . . . Some time ago my friends decided to play a merry prank on me, they told me that we were going to the home of certain lady friends of theirs, but instead I realized that the place was an infamous brothel. The girl they left me with stripped naked before me and said: 'Well, what are you waiting for? Take off everything you're wearing and let's have some fun!' But the minute I saw her naked, I took to my heels."

"Why, was she that ugly?"

"No, I don't think so . . . I didn't even really look at her all that closely, but it was just that I didn't like having to talk with a naked woman I'd never been introduced to."

"Well, in that case, since we've introduced ourselves, even if I stripped naked, would you still talk to me?"

"Oh my God . . . are you making fun of me?"

"Not at all! Come on, get busy, take your clothes off!"

"What are you saying?! Just like that? Here and now?"

"Yes, you're right: maybe we should get to know each other a little better first."

"Excuse me, but have you been with other men? How many?"

"Well, right here and now, I couldn't say . . . I'm kidding, of course! Do you want to know the truth? I'm married!"

"No! You mean that you have a husband?"

"No, I don't have a husband anymore. They forced me to marry him, for reasons . . . that I'm not going to tell you about.

But then my folks decided to get rid of him and they managed to dissolve the marriage, and so now I'm unmarried again, and all alone."

"And . . . how long were the two of you together, how long were you married?"

"I beg you—enough of this interrogation. There's something I've wanting to tell you for ages, since I helped you up off the floor and we embraced, and I looked at you, and you know what? You're the handsomest young man I've ever seen in my life. You told me that I seem like a queen to you, but to me you're handsomer than any king. I'd marry you right here and now. Just to make love with you."

"Oh my heavens! Are you serious?" The boy took a deep breath and then said: "So would I."

The next morning they woke up in each other's arms. They moved just slightly apart and lay there in silence gazing at each other, then she got to her feet on the large bed and exclaimed: "God! Seen from above and stark naked, you're even handsomer! To what house do you belong, Neapolitan?"

"I can't tell you, I'm not sure you'd like it if you knew, and in any case I'm not sure whether my father and his brothers would ever let me marry you."

"Stop worrying about it and just tell me what house you belong to."

"Aragon."

"Aragon! Good God! That's like saying the royal family of Naples."

"True, but I'm an illegitimate member of the house of Aragon."

"As far as that goes, I'm an illegitimate daughter myself."

"Of what house?"

"Of the house of Borgia."

"Borgia? Oh, sweet Mary mother of God!"

To follow the paths of heaven you need only be able
to read the movements of the stars

The pope was in his office with his back to the window, and he said in a loud voice: "Come on, come right on in, Gertrude! And have a seat."

The young nun entered the office and bowed: "You called me, Your Holiness?"

"Yes. I have a very serious job for you to do."

"I only hope that I'm able to do it properly. Tell me, Holy Father."

"Soon, I believe it will actually be today, we will have two visitors, very important individuals as far as I'm concerned. One of them is Polish, but he speaks good Italian, the other is from Ferrara and he is the Pole's teacher, even though the student has since become more famous than his master."

"That sort of thing happens, from time to time."

"True. The Pole is named Copernicus, and he's a scientist who studies the stars, while the other one is named Novara and he is not only an astronomer, he's also a mathematician, and he reads and speaks ancient Greek."

"My goodness, that would be so exciting for me, to meet such learned people."

"I have to say, it would be exciting for me, too. But let's talk about your job: you must make sure that the usual busybodies, and there are more than enough of them around here, don't stick their noses in the whole time that these two scholars are in here with me."

"As you wish, Holy Father, I'll go straight to the front door of the palazzo and alert the concierge to their arrival. Would you be so good, Your Holiness, as to repeat their names for me?" And with these words she pulled out a notebook and a pencil.

"No! Don't write anything!" said Alexander VI, stopping

her. "Memorize everything, I don't want to see notes any-where, of any kind. If you write a single word and it falls into their hands, and you know who I'm talking about, they will immediately start an investigation, followed by a trial."

"You're right, Your Holiness. If I may," and she left the room.

The pontiff went back to his desk, but almost immediately the nun came back into the room: "Forgive me, Holy Father."

"What is it, Gertrude, did you forget something?"

"No, Your Holiness, its just that the two scholars have arrived, they're climbing the stairs right now."

"Goodness, how quick they are! All right, go and meet them, greet them with the reverence befitting them, and lead them to me."

Not a minute went by before—behold!—the two scientists entered the pontiff's office; the pontiff stood up and walked toward them: "Welcome, welcome, my friends. You're here earlier than I expected you."

"Well, given how urgently you summoned us," said the elder of the two, "we made all possible haste."

"I would have to imagine that you," said the pontiff, point-ing to the man who had just spoken, "are Master Novara and that he, the young man, is your pupil, Copernicus. Did I guess right?"

"Yes, that's us."

"Make yourselves comfortable."

The nun hastened to push forward two chairs, then she went to the far side of the room and stood next to the door. As he sat down, Master Novara said: "Forgive me, Your Holiness, but before we begin our conversation, we'd like to know why you've chosen to ask us of all people, a pair of astronomers, for advice on how to solve a problem that might have crucial repercussions on the future of Christendom."

Nicolaus Copernicus

"Let me answer with a question. How did you know that this is a crucial problem for me and for the future of the church?"

"That's simple," the Pole replied. "You're forgetting that by now all of Italy is talking about this project of yours, as is every country in Europe."

"The only thing is," added Novara, "we can't figure out why you would want to use two scientists who, by their instincts and training, tend to have their heads in the universe much more than on the problems here on earth."

"First and foremost, because of what you yourself admitted: it is your job to read the stars, and so you are closer to God than most. You see, there is an ancient saying in Catalonia, where I come from: 'If you want to know how to act in difficult circumstances, you can ask a sorcerer, who might consult the viscera of a slaughtered hen, or a witch, who might feel the pulse in your temples while peering into your eyes, but best of all, this you must believe, is to ask those who read the stars.' What's more, one of you, certainly Master Novara, rounds out the living he makes as an astronomer by working as an astrologer as well, which means that he can predict anyone's future by conversing with astral bodies."

Practically in chorus the two scholars replied: "It's true, forgive us for our curiosity."

The pope went on: "Now, let's come to the subject of us. Since you're already well informed about the decision that I announced in the most recent consistory concerning the transformation—it's fair to say the total transformation—of the entire ecclesial structure, I'd be curious to know what you thought of it."

"To tell the truth," Novara replied, "we had a hard time getting a copy of that program of yours, and when we read it we were both struck and baffled."

"I beg you to speak freely and explicitly, we don't have

much time. Moreover, unfortunately, since we began the process of assembling this structure we've had to be aware of the many creakings and mutterings and even a few partial but fairly significant collapses, none of which bode well for the future."

"Well, Your Holiness, that's as normal as can be, when trying to implement as far-reaching a transformation as yours."

And here the young Pole spoke up in his turn: "If you'll forgive me, Holy Father, I find the project unbalanced, to say the least."

"What is that supposed to mean?"

"In physics that's a term we use to describe something that imposes a paradox of equilibrium, an impulse of total transformation, that is to say, anything that definitively spills outside of the canons of normality."

"Very nice, I like that definition! But, to come back to the project, do you consider it to be possible or utopian?"

Master Novara, with a strange smile, boldly replied: "Holy Father, unfortunately we are going to have to ask you to be patient and wait for the sun to set and night to fall, because it is difficult to read the stars in the light of day."

The pope couldn't hold in his laughter, and said, in his amusement: "Ha ha ha! That's a rich one, at first I didn't get it."

"Excellent!" exclaimed the young Pole. "It is our good luck to have a pontiff with a sense of humor. We can rest easy, he won't denounce us to the tribunal of the Inquisition."

The pontiff showed that he could take that irony in stride and the conversation went on.

"Forgive me, Your Holiness," Copernicus went on, "just a short while ago you spoke of creakings and mutterings and open opposition on the part of your colleagues and advisers who, evidently, are contrary to, or at least doubtful about, the possibility of undertaking such an operation, am I right?"

"Yes, that's exactly it."

Master Novara

"In that case," Master Novara quickly replied, "it is clear that right here and now you realize that you do not yet fully possess the dialectical power needed to defy those negative observations and that resistance."

"Yes, that's more or less accurate."

"And therefore you are turning to us in the hope that we might help you to find powerfully persuasive words."

"Excellent, very nicely put."

"But in order to do that," Copernicus concluded, "we'd need you to tell us exactly what forms of opposition you're having a hard time breaking down . . . "

"I," said the pontiff, clearly enunciating every word he spoke, "have set as the fundamental target of our program, first and foremost, a scraping away of the incomes and especially of the privileges that are enjoyed by bishops, cardinals, and all those who manage the church's assets. In the second place I have ordered that no one dare continue to exploit sources of certain enrichments of the church, such as the giving of charity, for instance."

"Let us stop then and analyze these two points, if you don't mind, Your Holiness," the young scientist interrupted him. "What did your opponents reply concerning the scraping away of paychecks, if you'll forgive me for being flippant?"

"They declared themselves decidedly opposed to it. First of all they reminded me that their duty is to collect tithes and donations, and also, to manage responsibly the properties that are the appanage of the curia itself: 'We are servants of God, we can't think of exploiting those who care for His vineyard!' And that wasn't all: another cardinal, a moderate and thoughtful person, added: 'I would gladly don tattered, ragged clothing, I'd happily eat cheap and poorly cooked food out of wooden bowls, but how can I meet and invite authorities of the secular world to my pauper's table? To say nothing of foreign princes? *Please, be seated, Your Majesty, would you care for a bowl of beans with root vegetables from my fields and a quail's egg? I certainly hope it's still fresh!'"*

"Well, that was certainly to be expected," exclaimed the young Pole. "The bishops have been accustomed to these privileges for centuries now. I was just reading the other day a chronicle of the Nicene Council in the year A.D. 325, and it made me understand where and how the church was transformed from a poor and persecuted community to the Holy Roman Church at the service of the empire."

"How very odd!" Alexander VI said, as he burst out laughing. "I believe that's the same anthology of accounts that I read myself no more than a month ago, and let me assure you that it was crucial to my composition of this draft reform. One of the passages that struck me most forcefully was the list that one of the contributors, a bishop of Rome, drew up of the Christian martyrs of the three previous centuries. A fullfledged slaughter, he said, of poor wretches ripped limb from limb in the arenas, prophets nailed on crosses, head-up or head-down, women raped, children hurled off cliffs. And at this point a voice was raised: 'Enough, enough, we can't go on like this. If we choose to reject the protection of the powerful at every turn we shall certainly become the world's most respected religious movement, but not long after that we shall entirely become members of the holy and pure community of the deceased.'"

"Perfect!" Novara responded. "I see, Your Holiness, that you've practically memorized that passage. And without a doubt you must also remember the edict of Constantine, both the authentic one and the counterfeit."

"No, I didn't read that part with sufficient attention."

"Well," Copernicus commented, "allow me to remind you of it. Constantine said: 'The bishops who voted for the transformation into a protected church managed to obtain extraordinary privileges. First and foremost, they won respect and consideration in the eyes of the established power, to a degree that would have been unimaginable before that. They obtained for the first time, at the end of the Council of Nicaea, subsidies from the empire, the right to gather money, even in the form of taxes, fertile lands with rivers running through them, temples to pagan gods transformed into places of Catholic worship and, last of all, hear ye, o hear ye, the right to employ servants and even, in certain cases, slaves.'"

"Well, at this point we can safely say that Christianity has wandered very far from the apostles and from Christ, but we can also say that Christ, I am afraid, has moved far away from us."

"Lord, Lord!" Copernicus exclaimed. "But are we really sure, and I say this with the utmost respect, that the person we hear speaking these words to us right now really is the pontiff, the father of the Catholic church?"

"I can tell you," Novara confessed in something close to a whisper, "that as a result of the experience of talking to princes of the church over the years, I've moved sharply away from the faith I once held, but right now I can assure you that, if I really were to see the rebirth of a community of Christians like what I seem to understand you hope to build, I would be among your most fervent supporters." And at that point the Holy Father got to his feet and began to pace back and forth in his study, in order to marshal his thoughts.

At a certain point he stopped and, looking up, said: "Do you know what I think? It's impossible to reconstruct a new building by trying to restore a building whose foundations can no longer support the structure. The appearance is still impressive, but it's inconceivable to transform it into something new."

"Just what is that supposed to mean?" exclaimed Copernicus. "That the only reasonable response would be to demolish the building entirely and rebuild it from the ground up?"

"Exactly. We say that the Roman empire 'collapsed,' but what has been rebuilt is far worse than what was there before.

And why is that? Because it was rebuilt starting from the same old foundations. Therefore, when we say 'rebuild from the ground up,' that ground must be cleared entirely, starting over from absolute zero."

"Yes, but in order to succeed in such an operation, there's something else that would have to change first," Novara declared.

"What is that?" asked the pontiff.

"Mankind. If the rebuilders express the same thoughts, habits, rules, and behaviors as those who have been swept aside, or if they are the same people as before, palmed off as innovators, then you're always going to be rebuilding the same old things."

"Well then?"

"Well then, if we're not capable of demolishing ourselves in order to rebuild ourselves, then the only thing to do is to remain exactly as we are. Any other solution may seem extraordinary, but it won't do a bit of good."

Naples is beautiful during the day in the hottest sunshine,
by night with or without the moon, but better than anything
else, Naples is magnificent to behold if you're in love

These are the words of a song that young Alfonso of Aragon dedicated to Lucrezia the very day that his beautiful bride-to-be first came to see him. The young man had talked his father, King Alfonso II of Naples, into consenting to this relationship, and he had done so with the assistance of Cesare Borgia. The pope's son immediately got to work as soon as Lucrezia confided that she'd fallen head-over-heels in love with the young man. He'd personally requested an audience with the king of Naples in order to intercede in favor of the two young people, in his father's name as well as his own.

In the meantime, Alexander VI had begun with calm and detachment to braid the colored threads of the tapestry that would tell the tale of the slowly evolving saga of the failure of a project to transform from top to bottom the Roman Catholic church. Taking great care, in the midst of that collapse, to land on his feet, unhurt.

As he planned how to weave the warp and woof of his upcoming conversations with the leading cardinals in the consistory, he asked himself how he could have ever hoped to undertake such a profound transformation when the individuals who were being asked to put it into effect were the very same cunning and hypocritical scoundrels against whom that reform was designed. Those men's hands were already plunged far too deep into the pockets of businessmen and manufacturers who required the approval of the curia to carry out their projects. The customs of fraud and deceptive practices were certainly not about to be shaped and transformed for the better thanks solely to new laws and innovative regulations. By now Pope Rodrigo had grasped the lesson. It was a complete waste of time to worry about improving the living conditions inside a sand castle built on the beach while waiting for the waves of an unusually high tide to sweep the whole thing away, along with its builders. He would have to act with great caution and shrewdness. And he'd have to remember that in politics postponement is always a winning strategy: postponement in fact is one of the fundamental resources available to programs that cannot, or perhaps should not, be undertaken.

The hardest thing for Alexander VI was getting past the stumbling block of the "morality" issue. That is, how was he to modify, at least in appearance, his licentious need for forbidden copulation? For that matter, how on earth could anyone keep their distance from such an adorable creature as Giulia? An old saying goes: "If the hyenas are on your heels, then toss them the most savory morsel, say, a newborn lamb. You'll see, when they open their maws to savage their prey, there's not a hyena or jackal on earth that will pay the slightest attention to anything else."

And so the great reformation was gently lowered into the swamp of forgetfulness. Every so often someone with a good memory would ask: "When are we going to talk about that revolution again?"

And everyone, from the pontiff down to his cardinals, would reply: "Never fear, we haven't forgotten. Just be patient and we'll bring it back up again."

Sure, and who believed them?

Lovers' quarrels

Lucrezia is in Rome. The scene opens in the very instant at which the thump of the door knocker is heard at the bottom of the central staircase and the voice of a servant girl calls: "Milady, it is your lover who just knocked on the door!" And Lucrezia responds: "At last! What are you waiting for? Let him in!"

"He's already entered, that's him on the stairs!"

Alfonso appeared, she hurried toward him to throw her arms around him, and he pushed her away.

"Hey, what's come over you? Why do you shove me away?"

"Why don't you ask your brother and your father, too! You're a fine gang of blackguards!"

"Blackguards? Why, are you drunk or are you just pretending to insult me?"

"Listen, you're a woman of letters, do you like ballads and *strambotti*? Then why don't you just try reading this!" And with those words, he pulled a sheaf of paper from inside his jacket. "Be my guest, it's dedicated to you, or really, I should say, to us both. It's funny as can be."

The girl grabbed the sheets of paper and asked: "Who wrote these words?"

"It was a certain Bellomo Quattronateche, he's a buffoon of course! *Spassoso assai.* A very funny man."

"Now what, are you speaking Neapolitan to put me ill at ease?"

"Putting you ill at ease? Why, who can do that? Enough with the whining! Just listen to what he has to say." He ripped the paper out of her hands and began to read, carefully enunciating each word in Neapolitan dialect: "How lovely you are, Lucrezia, and sweet, and how your eyes are like those of angels, but you also act with impunity and you play the part of a lover in a company of rogues and scoundrels, and so you have turned this young man, that is, me, a king's half-nephew, into a gape-jawed idiot, you've talked him into believing that the two of you met by chance, while instead the whole thing was carefully planned out, he was the only one to know nothing about it. So the two of them have suddenly fallen so in love they could die. Instead the whole thing was planned cold-bloodedly by her brother, Big Cesare, the bandit chief, and by her holy father, while the king of Naples was in on the scheme. They'd all worked out the contract even before the two of them met. And this poor fool of a boy was convinced that they were meeting because the goddess Fortuna, who is also the goddess of love, had wished it. Ah, what ridiculous crap!"

Lucrezia burst into tears. And the young man burst out laughing.

"Ah, of course, we were bound to come to tears! Weep and sob, and in the meanwhile make a fool out of the idiot!"

"That's enough out of you!" shouted Lucrezia, and gave him a good hard slap. "I don't know anything about this, understood?"

"Oh, yes? And your brother, Cesare, he doesn't know anything either? Your father, or Adriana, your pandering nurse?

Just for starters, let me tell you that I practically assaulted my father, and in response all he did was burst out laughing. 'Oh, at last!' he shouted. 'You figured out what we were scheming behind your back! But what do you care if you were convinced that it was all by accident? The young lady is a real beauty, she has enough money to get a banker drunk, and you'll get a nabob's dowry out of it. And in the end you'll be the pope's own son-in-law, and your son might, someday, even become king of Naples. And you, Lucrezia, will be queen! You see the machinations?"

"I don't know anything about it at all, I tell you! I swear it!"

Just then, the servant girl stuck her head through the door and said in a hushed voice: "Milady, your brother is about to come in, he just dismounted from his horse! What shall I do?"

"Thank you, now you take Alfonso up to the mezzanine, and take him directly overhead, where there's a round hole from which he can see everything that's happening in here without being seen, and more importantly, where he can eaves-drop. Go on, take him upstairs!"

And as the servant girl led him up another staircase, Lucrezia told him loud and clear: "Listen carefully to how Cesare replies to the things I say to him."

The two leave the room, Lucrezia sits down at a loom that stands in the middle of the room, and begins moving the shuttle.

"Oh, Lucrezia! I'm happy to find you at home! But what is this, don't you even say hello to me?"

"And why should I? For the way you continue to make use of me, what should I do? Thank you kindly, perhaps?"

"I don't see what you're driving at."

"Listen, did you know that in Naples in certain streets there are storytellers who describe the lovers' tryst between me and Alfonso, and they laugh heartily as they do so?"

"What are you talking about?"

"All right, it may be that you know nothing about storytellers, so let me give you a chance to broaden your education. Read this." And she threw the pamphlet with the ballad at his feet. "It's in Neapolitan, do you know Neapolitan? Well, if you don't, here's your chance to learn it, it will prove useful if you really want to become king of Naples . . . "

Cesare read it and after scanning half a page, exclaimed: "Why, what kind of buffoonery is this?"

"It's our kind, my dear, and therefore it's first-rate buffoonery!"

"Well, what do you have to complain about? Haven't you always berated us indignantly, decrying the fact that we used you as a pawn in the larger chess game of our vested interests? And now that we're doing everything within our power to let you choose the enchanted love affair you've long dreamed of, you still come pestering us, denouncing us as if your father and I were a couple of pimps?"

"Yes, it's true, I have no right to make these demands. You're right, I'm just an insatiable girl. You have moved heaven and earth to put reservations for me on two young men of the Spanish nobility . . . "

"And let it be clear, we obtained two so that if the first one didn't meet with your approval . . . "

"Then you reconsider and you decide that those two half-wits weren't worthy of me, and you discard them into the rubbish. Then you decide to find me an even better one, in fact, a young man from the House of Sforza! And what could be better than that? I might not love him, but you force me to accept him all the same. I adapt to the situation, I do everything within my power to like him and get along with him. For four years we live like lovebirds, certainly the fact that he's head over heels in love with me can't help but make me like him better, but then my father, in cahoots with you, decides that, no, he's no longer a worthy mate, and so you force us both to sign a document stating that we never consummated our marriage.

I finally find the man of my dreams, but then I discover that he was completely fabricated by the pair of you, there's nothing in my life that's happened by chance. In other words, I've just been acting a part in a play, and always to the best advantage of you and your interests!"

"Ah, I'm sick of you! Forgive me, eh, but I don't have any time to waste on your complaints. Why don't we talk again when you've had a chance to calm down. See you later!"

Cesare left, and a few moments later Alfonso came back downstairs, sat down next to his girl, and after a long silence said: "Forgive me for what I said, and for the way I insulted you."

"Don't worry, you had every right. Curse them . . . They just don't seem to be capable of stopping themselves from treating people like secondhand shoes."

"What now? What should we do?" Then, without waiting for a response: "I can't live without you. I'm in love."

"So am I. I adore you," she said. "You're in my life every moment of the day, even when you're not with me: when I sleep, when I walk down the street, when I eat. I eat you and I let you eat me."

"I like the idea of being your food and you being mine. Then let us remain together, let us protect each other from the world."

And she replied, almost instantly: "Careful, though, even if one of them is my brother and the other one is my father, by now I've learned not to trust them entirely, ever. Suffice it to consider how deceitfully this man who wants to be called the Holy Father behaved in the last consistory. I heard him with my own ears as he called on astonished bishops and cardinals to destroy all the rot that's bubbling away in the Vatican's kitchens. He even put together a council of righteous wise men, but the minute it became clear to him that he'd have to unleash a full-fledged war and battle every powerful group, he immediately doffed his lion skin and donned the hide of a shimmering chameleon. For that matter, the talent for meta-morphosing before your very eyes is an extraordinary prerogative of this kind of people. My brother, practically in unison with his father, immediately took off his purple silk vestments. He discarded his cardinal's biretta and with stunning speed the donned the armor, helmet, boots, and sword of a warrior prince."

"And all just so that he can more conveniently carry out his lurid business affairs . . . Certainly, we will never be able to sleep soundly. Forgive me for being brutal but you seem to have been born into… I couldn't say what… a toad's nest of horrendous creatures, for whom anyone who stands in the way of their plans can safely be said to be already dead."

"You are right. If we go along with their plans, we will always be at risk of being manipulated to their convenience and best interests."

They embraced and whispered, practically in unison: "Let us hope that this love of ours never ends."

The trading game

On October 1st, 1498, Cesare Borgia traveled to Paris. This was a city he did not know, but that he'd begun to love when he first learned the French language, a language that, as we saw during his trip to Naples in the entourage of King Charles VIII, he could speak well, with agility and fine style. But what was he going to do in a city so far from home? He had no less a mission than that of requesting the hand in marriage of Charlotte of Aragon; it is no accident that this Charlotte was also a cousin of Alfonso, who was now husband to Lucrezia, as well as the daughter of Frederick, King of Naples. But this was no happy end to a tender love story; it was an entirely political affair. By marrying a daughter of the house of Aragon, Cesare would find himself at least one very high step advanced on the stairway leading up to the throne of Naples.

But the meeting did not go at all as hoped. The sought-after bride, when she was apprised of the proposed union, attacked the matchmakers and threw a tantrum of violent indignation: "What? Are you suggesting I wind up between the sheets with a thug of that order? A certified assassin worthy of the worst brothels imaginable? Have you forgotten that he is the same bastard who took my cousin as his lover, stealing her away from her husband, who was none other than his own younger brother? What on earth can you be thinking? That I should give my hand in marriage to this infamous ruffian, who might very well take me to bed and then the next morning, after ravishing my virginity, cheerfully kill me as I sleep, like the murderous satrap in the *Arabian Nights*?"

Her refusal was brutal and unappealable, but Cesare didn't really take it that hard. As the saying goes, plot twists are like the winds that drive ships across the waters; when a sirocco turns into a strong cold mistral, then it's time to shift course. And what does a man like Cesare do when, in the midst of a chess match, he loses a queen? Why he quickly gets himself another. The Neapolitan queen said no, but it turned out there was also a young French noblewoman—as it happened, another Charlotte, Charlotte d'Albret, sister to the king of Navarre. She was willing, as was her father, so: Long live the newlyweds!

This chess move won him the sympathy of the king of France, Louis XII, and in truth Louis made shrewd use of the favor he had shown toward the pope's favorite son to win his support—the pope's support, we mean—for the annulment of his marriage. The French monarch had made an unsuccessful marriage with Joan of Valois, a young woman who was mentally ill. Only the pope could put an end to this marriage. Moreover, the king was seeking the Vatican's approval for a project that was dear to his heart—the conquest of the king-dom of Naples. Even higher on his list of ambitious projects was the conquest of Milan. For this bold undertaking, the French king appointed Cesare as his lieutenant, which meant that the young man finally had an army at his disposal, an army that he would lead in cooperation with the monarch to attack not only Milan, but also a number of other important cities in Romagna.

Milan was conquered, after which the armies moved south into Romagna.

A few months later, on February 26, 1500, Cesare marched into Rome as a victorious condottiere. His father had readied for him a triumph befitting an emperor, and went so far as to appoint him gonfalonier of the church. But the most festive and jubilant welcome was that accorded him by the people of Rome. In particular the clerks of the city's public administration greeted the pope's son with feverish acclaim. In fact, the feudal lords of Romagna had long been a grievous burden to the Papal State. Troublesome and ungovernable, they had refused for years to pay the taxes they rightly owed the government of Rome, which was therefore obliged to take that shortfall out on the inhabitants of the Eternal City, and in particular on the city's employees who hadn't seen their salaries in months. Borgia's victory meant, to them, the certainty that they would soon see their back pay in the form of substantial lump sums.

In his official welcome of Cesare, the "holy" father was forced to keep his own pleasure and pride in such a joyously acclaimed son to a minimum. But once they were finally alone in the papal palace, Rodrigo embraced his son so passionately that Cesare could hardly breathe. Then, as the papal butlers were serving lunch to a table at which sat only father and son, Alexander VI exclaimed, expressing himself in his native Catalan: "Tell me all about this triumph of yours!"

And the son replied, also in Catalan: "Just let me catch my

breath for a moment, *pare*, because I'm as overwhelmed as you are by the joy of this reception."

"Yes, of course, catch your breath, but then tell me everything. Start at the beginning and don't leave out a thing, from the moment the King of France appointed you his right-hand man."

And Cesare began the narrative, pushing his place setting aside on the table so that he would have more room to tell the story of his adventures and gesticulate while doing so: "Well, let me start by telling you, *pare meo*, that the first expedition, the conquest of Milan, was really the acid test for me. I'd come to know the city like the back of my hand ever since the time you sent me there to lay the preparations for the wedding of our Lucrezia to Giovanni Sforza, that pusillanimous miscreant, who we justifiably chased out of our family. And so, when King Louis asked my advice as to the best way to take on Ludovico the Moor and his troops, I answered him, taking care not to seem overweening: 'In my opinion this will be for you the easiest siege of a city that could be hoped for.' 'Thanks to what advantage, pray tell?' 'Thanks to the very advantages that the Duke of Milan has created for us with his own hands, for he, by behaving like a foolish lout, has quickly lost whatever repute he began with, to such a degree that there is not one subject left in that city who does not madly desire to rid himself not only of the duke, but of all his court and every one of his henchmen.' Whereupon the king, deeply intrigued, asked me: 'Why? Just what has this boastful varlet done wrong?' 'Nothing could be simpler, he has thought only of his own interests. He hasn't even pretended to show concern for the needs of his people.' In short, the very opposite of what you have always taught me, *meo pare*: he who looks to his own interests and at the same time those of his people will always land on his feet, and the people, from the most tattered paupers up, will adore him. Let us say nothing, of course, of how he will be beloved by the most prominent members of society."

"Yes, *Sèsar*. But he must also take care not to let the most prominent citizens gain the upper hand: the minute they sense even a hint of weakness in those who wish to win their favor, they will strip you naked, and no king can ever allow himself to be seen in his undergarments!"

"I could not agree more, but to come back to my conversation with the king of France, I reminded him that Ludovico the Moor had gone too far with his promises: 'Milanesi!' he said to them in a booming voice. 'My beloved subjects! Now that you have taken me as your duke, I assure you that I will rebuild your city, I will sweep it clean of the gangs of profiteers and the banks, which can no longer even be called institutes of credit, but rather institutes of loan-sharking, and most important of all I will restore to good working order the canals and rivers. Moreover, I will order the restoration of the sewers which, as I have been publicly told by no less a personage than Leonardo da Vinci, are overrun with rats that venture boldly everywhere, even into the city's churches during wedding ceremonies.' And at this point I told the king: 'All you need do, Your Majesty, is present yourself alone before the walls of Porta Romana and you shall see that the gates will swing open and the entire populace will come forth cheering and calling your name.'"

"And how did the king react to this prediction of yours?"

"At first he seemed skeptical but then, given the way things actually turned out, he was forced to admit that I, his lieutenant, had predicted events with great precision. And when we marched into Milan, he insisted that I stay close by his side, arm in arm, the way *you* do, at least when you remember that I am your son."

His father laughed briefly and added: "Now, don't wander off track, we've come to the point where you enter Romagna with your troops. Tell the rest!"

"The story is soon enough told. We marched on the cities

of Imola and Forlì, but there our armies unexpectedly encountered ferocious resistance and even had to face down a powerful counterattack by the local troops, led to my astonishment by a woman, Caterina Sforza, a female endowed with extraordinary fortitude and charisma. Just think: she managed to stir in her subjects a pride befitting a genuine race of warriors. We had quite a struggle in persuading her to surrender so we could take her prisoner!"

Omens of disaster

Now it was June 26 and it was the heart of summer. Alexander VI found himself subjected to an ill omen that descended on him from on high. An enormous chandelier in his throne room broke away from its moorings to the ceiling and dropped straight down onto the papal throne just as the pope stood up to retrieve a small gold coin that had slipped through his fingers. To his horror, the pope realized that he had cheated death by fractions of an inch. And thanks to a small gold coin.

But this was only the first warning. In fact the very next day (and it was one of the very few days in which Cesare was absent), Alexander VI was about to begin a papal audience in the throne room, when the sky exploded with thunder and lightning that sounded like the end of the world. There was a brief silence, followed by a thunderstorm befitting the Last Judgment. Then came a series of loud cracks and the beams supporting the roof suddenly collapsed. Upright beams and tie rods plummeted down onto a heap of rubble. Two cardinals saved themselves by dashing for the recess of a window. Alexander VI sat motionless on his throne, under the baldachin that fell atop him.

Almost immediately word of the disaster spread through

the city. Despairing voices wailed out, over and over: "He's dead! The pope has been killed, crushed under a collapsing roof!" Men set to work to extract the corpse but, to their immense surprise, when they found him seated on his throne, beneath the shattered arches of the baldachin, he was unconscious but still very much alive.

At the Holy Father's bedside there was no one but his daughter. He had personally given orders that he was to be attended by Lucrezia and no one else.

The evening of July 15, 1500, seemed to be immersed in peace and complete quiet. Alfonso of Aragon was climbing the last steps leading to the four-sided portico of Saint Peter's when he was attacked by several masked individuals who converged on him brandishing long daggers. The young man managed to leap out of their grasp, but he wasn't quick enough to keep one of them from lunging forward and stabbing him in the arm. He staggered. It was about eleven at night and there was only the dimmest of light from the lamps fastened to the façade of the archways. One of the ruffians caught up with him and gave him a thump on the back of the head.

There was someone only a few paces away who saw the ambush, but he took great care not to intervene or sound the alarm. He simply melted into the shadows. Alfonso managed to escape again and kicked viciously at the nearest assassin, but the killer stabbed him deeply in one leg. Alfonso fell to the ground. The three killers saw a platoon of guards rushing toward them and shouting threats, whereupon the ruthless killers took to their heels. The platoon reached the stairs and immediately the first two guards kneeled over the unfortunate victim and saw that he was still breathing. Four of them picked him up and carried him through the portico to the entrance of the basilica and the guard barracks. There the captain recognized the young man and exclaimed: "By God, this is the son-in-law of His Holiness the Pontiff!"

Still running as fast as their legs would carry them, the four guards carried the wounded man into the inner rooms of the Vatican where Lucrezia Borgia lived. The lady hurried toward the rescuers. When she realized that they were carrying her husband and that he was copiously bleeding she fell to the floor in a dead faint. They summoned a physician who stitched up the unfortunate victim's wounds as best he could and commented: "Fortunately the dagger blows failed to strike any vital organs. Unfortunately he's lost a great deal of blood. But he's young, and he may still make it. Now let us to see to her ladyship."

They managed to bring Lucrezia to, with the administration of smelling salts. The doctor took her pulse and declared: "She has a high fever, undoubtedly an effect of the great shock."

The black moon often rises twice

The next day, starting at dawn, outside the entrance to the suite of rooms where Lucrezia lived, there were two armed guards standing sentinel in the hallway at all times. The doctor was leaving the room where Alfonso lay wounded. Lucrezia was accompanying him with a baby in her arms.

"How is he doing? What a lovely son you have, he looks like one of those cherubs they paint around the Virgin Mary during her assumption into heaven."

And as Lucrezia kissed and petted her child, she replied: "He's the only member of this family who's still in good health."

"How old is he?" asked the physician.

"He was born nine months ago."

"Goodness gracious, congratulations! He looks as if he's a

year old, at least. Forgive me if I butt into matters that are none of my business, but do you have any suspicions as to who might have been responsible for this attack?"

"Two so-called masters of justice came this morning. They were sent by my father. Of course, they've already begun an investigation. All I've done all morning long is answer their questions. Allow me to express an opinion that by rights I ought to keep to myself: it seemed to me that the two of them knew far more about this unsuccessful assassination than what little they were pretending to find out from me."

"Perhaps you wouldn't remember, you were so over-wrought at the time, but I'm the same doctor that cared for you when you lost your first baby."

"Oh, please forgive me! Unfortunately at the time I was quite mad with grief."

"Eh, I remember . . . You were walking downstairs and you fell, and so you lost your first little one. A miscarriage in your third month, you had every right to be heartbroken. But then, just a short time later, I was pleased to see that you had recovered beautifully, and in fact, overjoyed, you told me: 'Doctor, I'm pregnant again.'"

And Lucrezia replied: "But my joy didn't last long, because my husband was almost immediately forced to flee, or should I say, he was persuaded to, by one of the cardinals in my father's entourage."

"Again, forgive me, perhaps I shouldn't inquire, but since I've heard so many different versions of this story, which one is true?"

"The truth has always been in my brother's hands. The cardinal, whose name I can tell you—Ascanio Sforza—came to see my husband Alfonso and warned him: 'You are in grave danger, my young friend, someone from your, shall we say, acquired family wishes to put a brutal end to your life. Listen to me, flee as fast as you can to what safety you can find,' and

Alfonso retorted: 'There are no safe places where I can hide.' 'In that case, go to my estate in Genazzano, there is a fortified castle there. No one even dares to set foot there, I have so many armed men at my disposal.' And so, from one day to the next, I found myself about to give birth, completely alone. I wept for days at a time. Fortunately the child never suffered any harm."

"And so for the whole time you were pregnant you never once saw your husband again?"

"Yes, that's exactly right."

"Still, and again forgive me for prying, why did your family ... why did your brother mean to kill your husband after doing everything within his power to arrange for you to marry him?"

"I know that this must strike you as a horrible thing, but among the males of the Borgia family, this habit of changing plans after putting them into effect is entirely normal, and since the fastest way to make that happen involves murder, that solution is generally the one chosen. In this specific case, my marriage was not the ultimate goal of the project, but rather the intermediate one. My brother, as usual all on his own, had decided that Naples might be a kingdom best conquered through the system of intermarriages. The first move in that game would be me, and with my marriage I would lay the cornerstone of the strategic takeover of that kingdom. Then I would be followed by Cesare, who would make his entry by making his intentions known, as the phrase would have it, toward my husband's fair cousin, and thus ascend the throne of Naples. But, as we all know, Charlotte of Aragon indignantly rejected the pretender's courtship."

"Ah! Now I understand! In that case," the physician exclaimed, "once he lost his chance at winning the kingdom of Naples for himself, your marriage to the young Aragon no longer served any purpose."

"Certainly, that's it. And so my husband became a spouse to be discarded. Into a grave, of course."

"Into a grave . . . which explains the reason for this attack, which fortunately did not prove fatal."

"Yes, but alas, I'm afraid that they'll try again."

"But how can that be? Unless I'm mistaken, your father, or perhaps I should say, your Holy Father, is openly protecting you. Around this house of yours, there is a ring of armed guards at every corner and in every nook and cranny."

"Yes, but that's not enough. Even if the aforementioned Holy Father has threatened to punish anyone who might dare to commit violence in our home, if I know Cesare, we should always fear the worst."

In fact, the following month Lucrezia's brother and some of his thugs broke into the house where she and her sister-in-law were caring for the convalescent young man. They brutally expelled the two women from the room and Captain Miguel de Corella, known as Michelotto, Cesare's personal assassin, entered Alfonso's room and in a flash choked him to death.

And here, just like in the Italian improvised theater of the Commedia dell'Arte, the game of masks begins its dance. Everyone takes part and performs their role, as well as the role of their antagonist. First the father claims to be indignant, then he turns a blind eye and preaches peace. The murdering son swears that he has committed no criminal deed, he acted purely in self-defense, because the victim dared to threaten him and even tried to shoot him with crossbow bolts. But the most upsetting aspect is the fact that after such a brutal attack, one which caused the subjects of other nations to explode in indignation, in Rome, in the era of Humanism, in the aftermath of that murder there was an atmosphere thick with a sort of slimy amalgam that made everything weightless and shapeless. Sheer oblivion.

Lucrezia encountered it firsthand: normally, she was frequently invited by friends who were only too happy to have her as a guest on all sorts of occasions; now she felt like an awkward outsider whenever she was with them, especially if she made any reference to the violence suffered. Everyone tried to avoid the subject and, since the young widow frequently exploded into words and deeds of indignation when she encountered that avoidance, she was eventually forced, day after day, to come to the realization that no one could stand to be around her anymore. As Aretino put it, "Heartbroken sobbing is only acceptable when the widow producing it is a matron whose power can bring benefits, or indeed is crucial to the lives of the courtiers. But if a ruler has already lost most of their power, then their laments simply become an intolerable wailing."

Lucrezia could no longer stand that agglomeration of cynicism that was Rome, where Cesare, by now, ruled over one and all. And so she willingly followed her father's exhortation to leave the Eternal City with her court and go to Nepi, a feudal holding that, importantly, belonged to her, where the air and the surroundings would surely redound to her benefit. In the midst of all that confusion the child grew up alert and energetic and increasingly tied by bonds of overwhelming affection to his mother.

But our readers should not believe that Lucrezia was abandoned by her father and brother to live in eternal isolation in that tiny fairy-tale city whose dimensions, unfortunately, were suited only to children. Alexander VI keenly felt the harsh responsibility of having reduced his daughter to a melancholy, indeed, a despairing widow, bereft of a young man that she had loved as she never again loved anyone else on earth. And he did all he could to free her from those straits. He loved her, he would have sacrificed his life to give his daughter happiness. This is the classic moral foundation of a tyrant: in the pursuit of their own interests they are always merciless and criminal, but when it comes to family ties they suffer and despair with all the passion of an authentic human being.

The sincere portrait of a people

Let us examine, as a commentary on all that happened, the analysis offered by Marion Johnson, an English historian of great learning and acuity, who tells the story of Italy in the Renaissance with the ruthlessness typical of the most brilliant British scholars: "Many were the laments throughout the fifteenth century on the state of Italy. Yet in this land where wits were quickened to a degree unknown in the rest of Europe, and where the study of history had been ordered into the beginnings of science, wise men knew very well that the fault came from within, lying in the life and the people." That is: in the subjects. "What Alexander VI and his son Cesare attempted was nothing more than the logical consequence of Italian political art. Their ends and their means were universally recognized, being in the tradition of Italian despotism. For several centuries the independent states of Italy had formed an arena in which any experiment was possible, and in which any man with talent, ruthlessness and an unquenchable thirst for fame could rise. As a result, Italian rulers had shown a sagacity, judgment, flexibility, and artistic impulse beyond the reach of any king or prince in the slovenly north; but all was allied to a cunning, faithlessness, cruelty and immorality beyond the comprehension of colder, more conservative peoples."[3]

[3] *Ibid.*, page 143.

The settling of accounts . . . to say nothing of privileges

As if to confirm the words of Marion Johnson, we have the contents of the missive sent by the pontiff to all the feudal lords of the Papal State: in it Alexander VI declared every one of them dismissed as rulers of their feudal holdings. What's more, he excommunicated them en masse, adducing as justification their failure to pay the taxes owed in arrears to the Papal State. Thus Cesare found himself, as was customary to say in Romagna, "lunching on butter and anchovies." And now, in fact, with astonishing ease, he managed in short order to overthrow the count of Pesaro, the Malatesta clan, lords of Rimini, the Montefeltros of Urbino, the Manfredis of Faenza, and the Varanos in Camerino. In other words, in short order he took possession of the entire region, including the numerous fortresses and castles. This exploit was greeted with amazement from one end of the peninsula to the other and throughout much of Europe. It was as a result of this successful campaign that Machiavelli commented with such enthusiasm that it might be possible, on the basis of what was happening in Romagna, to found a unified state in Italy. Hence his dedication to Cesare of his treatise on political doctrine, *The Prince*.

All roads, even the most impassable ones, lead to Rome

It was during that same period that the pope requested a meeting with his daughter, who by now had literally sought refuge in Nepi, but Lucrezia replied: "I'm sorry, but I'm unwilling to travel to Rome, especially because I'm so profoundly disgusted by the very thought of chancing to encounter, as would be customary, my brother Cesare, whom everyone now calls the slaughterer."

The pope's response came immediately. No longer than it took for a courier with two changes of horses to bring her this missive, with the following message: "Lucrezia, although you refuse to believe the things I say, I'm doing everything within my power to prove to you how much I love you. But it is rather complicated and challenging to achieve my intent. And therefore, in order to be successful, I will need your direct involvement. We cannot discuss this through letters and couriers. Come see me as soon as you can, I beg of you. As for your brother, I assure you that you will not see him in the short time you will spend here with me. For that matter, he is too engaged with his work in Romagna to be able to get away from that territory."

A few days later Lucrezia arrived in Rome. She fetched up not in the home she had shared with her husband, but in the palazzo of the Farnese family, as Giulia's guest. And she refused to meet her father in the Vatican. Too many painful memories kept her from returning to that location. At that point, the pope had a truly brilliant idea. In those days, they were excavating in Rome, one after the other, all the famous *domus* built by the most important Roman emperors. Alexander VI, mindful of how excited Lucrezia had been about the first discoveries of Nero's Domus Aurea, invited her to come tour the latest digs with him, and of course he arranged for all the numerous passionate art lovers to be kept away during their visit. They would be alone and undisturbed. Lucrezia accepted his invitation and there they met, in front of a painting of dancing fauns and nymphs.

There was a comfortable bench and they sat on it, side by side, and after a somewhat uncomfortable hug the conversation began. It was the pontiff who spoke first:

"Daughter of mine, first of all I should confess that in everything that has happened, the Borgia family has won great benefits. For all of us, save for you, Lucrezia. You alone, as if by some absurd decree of fate, have been forced to pay the price of our ruthless cunning, so often conducted with a wake of blood."

"These are honest words that you are finally saying to me, father. You've only forgotten to mention the name of the one who committed all these monstrous acts that I alone have been subjected to."

"He has not acted alone, my daughter. I, in my turn, admit my guilt, certainly, and I have suffered terribly. I will tell you that I have even considered eliminating Cesare from my life. But, I told myself, if left to his own devices this reckless son of mine will go on to commit who can say what increasingly horrific crimes, crimes that will take him to the brink of utter and total ruin, and he will take us with him ignominiously down into that abyss."

"Right. And so while we wait for the black sheep to turn a little whiter, I will continue to be ogled and described as a beguiling courtesan who allows her loving husbands to be cruelly eliminated, just because those marriages no longer fit in with the family's business interests."

"In fact," the pontiff exclaimed, "this is precisely the crux of the matter. Since I am responsible for your defamation, it is I who must do everything within my power to ensure that my daughter can regain her honorable name."

"And how are you planning to do that?"

"Forgive me, but allow me a question, Lucrezia: what city in Italy do you know best and love most?"

"Father, you really are a wily old fox. You ask a question to which you already know the answer. We've talked about it on other occasions. It's a place where I have spent unforgettable days, and it is called Ferrara."

"Very good. And why do you prefer that city over others?"

"Because the people there are sincerely likable and it seems to me that they have a great sense of community, along with a desire to live cheerfully and with respect for one and all."

"I couldn't agree with you more. Add the fact that the city has extraordinarily ornate palaces and that it is surrounded on all sides by the waters of the river Po, which has split itself in two in order to embrace it like a lover. The city is rich in markets, and merchants travel there from every corner of Europe. And it possesses a university, the Studio, where some of the greatest scientists, men of letters, and poets teach classes."

"I know all this. And add in as well the fact that it is perhaps the preeminent city in Italy as far as magnificent theatrical productions are concerned. There I have seen plays in the spoken tongue of an unimaginable magnificence. But excuse me, am I mistaken or is Ferrara exactly where you are suggesting I go to live?"

"Yes, that's right."

"And will I be able to choose for myself the friends that I prefer and a lover that suits me, or as usual have you already chosen a spouse?"

"Ah, behold, you have outplayed me and pushed me into a corner like a player cheating at lawn tennis. What a fool I am! I tangled myself up in my own nets like a rank beginner. But who did I think I was talking to? Didn't I know that my own daughter had learned the game of dialectics far better than her own teacher? So now what should I say?"

"Nothing other than the truth. Please do not equivocate with me as if you had some hope of catching me off guard with that cunning of the eternal winner of yours! You know, I was watching you as you spread your fishnets, I saw every step as you tightened the cords of your narrow-mesh traps, and I wondered the whole time: 'What is his game this time? Who is he planning to offer me to next in order to carry out his maneuvers?'"

"No, Lucrezia. At least in this case you've got it wrong! There is no maneuvering going on; I'm not striving after my personal advantage. At stake this time is my interest in placing you in a situation where you can be respected and considered at the very summit of social dignity. To do this, I'm willing to gamble money and my own credibility, I'm willing to involve highly placed persons, so that you can ascend to a place where no one will ever be able to show you any lack of respect again."

"I understand. I have no need of any further evidence or testimony. You've already sketched me a complete portrait of the person you have in mind for me. This is surely Alfonso, the son of Duke Ercole d'Este."

"Yes, perfect, that's him!"

"Does it occur to you that Alfonso is also the name of the man I loved more than any other and who a member of my own family murdered?"

"Yes, that's a horrendous coincidence. But what can I do about that? I beg of you, I'm having a hard time talking about this story. But I know that you've met him here in Rome, this Alfonso d'Este, though I don't know on what occasion. How did he look to you?"

"I didn't look at him all that carefully but, as the saying goes, never look a gift lover in the mouth."

"Actually, that's what they say about horses."

"You're right, and I'm not the one who would be riding this horse. In fact, I personally would find myself in the role of broodmare."

"In any case, give it some careful thought, I beg of you."

More or less at the same time, in Ferrara's Palace of Diamonds, now almost completed, a tempest was raging. One could tell by the fact that the large second-story windows were quickly being slammed shut, one after another. Clearly, someone was doing their best to keep shouting and stray words from being heard on the streets and in the palazzo across the way where a wedding feast was underway.

About to launch into a full-blown vociferous diatribe were

Ercole d'Este

Alfonso d'Este

none other than Duke Ercole d'Este and his firstborn son Alfonso. In fact, it was Alfonso who first lit the fuse of that *sparagnazzo*, as they say in Ferrara: "What do you take me for," he blurted, "some kind of dumb sucker you can gift wrap and sell under the counter to the first piece of trash to happen along?"

And Ercole retorted: "Well, if we're going straight for the insults, perhaps we'd better talk about something else!"

"Yes, that's better, it will allow us to avoid bad blood between us."

And the duke said: "Yes. Still, allow me to remind you that when you talk about another person, it's always a good rule to know who you're talking about, and not just rely on what 'people say' and 'it strikes me that.' "

"But father, that is exactly what I have done! I gathered information and I hired reliable people to carry out an investigation and bring me a report, and now here it is!" He pulled a sheaf of paper from a bag that he had set on the table. "I might say that I know practically everything there is to know about this delightful Lucrezia from the day of her birth until now. For years her father had delegated one of his henchmen to play the role of her mother's husband, and he paid him to serve in his stead as a parent to the girl and his three sons. Then the fake father died, and Cardinal Rodrigo procured another false father to replace the dead man. When one straw man vanishes, you get another to take his place. It was not until just before his election as Pope Alexander VI that the real father revealed to the entire family, except for the mother and the false bridegroom who already knew, that he was not an uncle as he had passed himself off for many years, but the actual father. And so the young girl learned that it was not with her uncle that she had been conducting an incestuous relationship, but with her father, a far more respectable and dignified affair!"

"Curse it all!" said Ercole slamming a fist down on the table. "Why, to what bordello ruffians have you gone to gather your information?"

"Certainly, certainly, it's far too filthy a tale to be accepted by well-mannered people like us! But what do you say about the fact that when she was just a girl, at age thirteen, she was married off to Giovanni Sforza, who was then twenty-four, that is, the same age I am now! And, poor little thing, she had to wait a year before she could consummate the marriage, because our laws forbid it at any younger age. Only at age fourteen can a young girl be legally deflowered! But the Holy Father changed his mind and forced the husband to acknowledge that he was impotent and drop the tidbit he'd been given. And notice this detail: after four years of unbroken and happy sexual relations! That's it, no more complaints, make way for the next customer! But after a while he too fell out of favor with the father and brother, to say nothing of the Holy Ghost! The only one who was pleased with him was her, and she adored him. And what do you do with a mighty tree that, as it grows, threatens to rip the roof off of your affairs? You chop it off at the roots. *Chop!* And so she was left a widow, but ready to be offered up to whom? *To me!* The village idiot! Oh, joy! Just what I've been waiting for all these years!"

"Alfonso, please, would you calm down for a moment and answer my questions? You tell me that you've already met this girl but that you haven't spoken to her, you've done nothing more than say a bland and generic hello. And so you know neither how she speaks nor her personality, whether she is a learned young woman or an uninteresting overgrown child . . . "

"I don't need to! If you don't mind, it was enough for me to read the menu of her copulations to decide whether she's the marrying kind or just a woman to spend the night with, strictly for the fun of it! And you, father, with the able assistance of your advisers, you'd like to arrange not only for us to go to bed together, but for her to become the mother of my children and of your grandchildren! Have you also taken into account the snickering scorn of our subjects, of bankers and merchants, to say nothing of the captains, knights, and even troops of infantry?"

"Certainly, certainly, and while you're at it, why don't you throw in the gossips, storytellers, buffoons, and tavern-goers in your sampling of public opinion? You see, unlike you I've actually taken the trouble to get to know her a little bit, that good woman whom you dismiss as a meretricious floozy. And I've written to her, asking her to come meet with me. A few days later, I received a letter from her that I supposed must be her reply, but in fact was sent a day before I mailed mine. And what did Lucrezia write to me? That she wished to meet with me, as discreetly as possible. And so I went to see her in person, in order to keep everything as understated as possible, in Nepi, at the far end of Umbria. And I spoke with her. For a whole day."

"What did you two have to say to each other?"

"In truth, more than anything else I listened to her, she did most of the conversing. She began by declaring: 'I will tell you, Your Excellency, that this nuptial project of yours is not notable for its clarity of purpose; it seems to have gotten off on the wrong foot, and if I may, the lame foot here is me.'"

"What a woman!" Alfonso d'Este commented sarcastically.

"Let me continue. Lucrezia went on to say: 'I think everyone sees me as a troublesome character, filled with dark patches which are for me the marks of a devastating grief. I have lived in conditions that have brought me to the point of wanting to end my life. To make a long story short, I entered a convent convinced I would stay there for good. But then I discovered that neither prayers nor penitence were sufficient for me to regain my equilibrium. I hated all the members of my family with a blind fury. Then a festive fate led me to meet a young man, just seventeen years old. I was one year older than him. We loved each other madly. I believe that such enchantment is a once-in-a-lifetime thing, and believe me, once can be enough.' Here she stopped to let me speak, and it took me some effort to reply: 'I'm very surprised, my lady,' I confessed. 'On my way here I hardly expected to meet a creature of the sincerity and honesty that you have so clearly displayed. And so, wishing to honor the atmosphere you have established, I will tell you in all honesty that I, in my turn, am also conditioned by my people, that is to say, by my family, which is sadly attached to the beliefs expressed in the most benighted and vulgar clichés and gossip. It is difficult, against such a background, to operate with simplicity and courage, and dispense unceremoniously with conventions and customs. The constant refrain is relentless: "How do you benefit from this? What is your immediate and personal profit? And how can you thwart the other side's inevitable efforts to swindle you and take everything for themselves?"'

'Certainly. The same thing happens to me whenever anything serious and momentous is at stake. Here too, I am like you, I carry on my back my own knapsack full of cunning ploys and a healthy helping of fraudulent ways. I could describe a few. And given the fact that—I say this without any attempt at adulation—I am speaking to man who possesses a noble soul and great learning, I can't help but feel I should reveal at least a few hidden phases of this negotiation process. First of all, let me say that the Holy Father, who also happens to be my own father, is playing to win. Thanks to you, thanks to your reputation for being a man who knows how to run a city with such wisdom that one and all can see it is a veritable masterpiece— thanks to you, I was saying, thanks to your willingness to take me into your family, I can now be seen by everyone as a brand-new woman.'

'Ah, dear Lucrezia, you have the power to stir my soul.'"

"If you go on like this for much longer, I'm going to roll on the floor and start sobbing!" Alfonso spat out contemptuously, while pretending to wipe tears from his eyes with the sleeve of his jacket.

"Alfonso, wait before ridiculing what you don't understand. Before long, if you are patient and listen to me, you really will be dabbing at your tears. And wiping your mouth as well."

The younger d'Este fell silent. His father continued relating the words Lucrezia had spoken to him:

"'But to conclude, there are still a few twists to this story that I absolutely ought to reveal. In the parlance of con games and extortion there's only one word for them: blackmail.'

'What kind of blackmail are you talking about?'

'Here's the first. The idea of wheedling you, my dear duke, whether or not you wish it, into accepting this risky marriage, and if you refuse, to put you in an awkward position.'

'And how would that be?'

'Well, for instance, by catching you off guard with the news that the contract by which you rule the duchy of Ferrara has been irrevocably rescinded. Never forget that it all lies within the jurisdiction of the pontiff, who, from one day to the next, without warning, has full power to choose whether or not to renew that lease or break it.'

'True. That particular sword of Damocles has been dangling uncomfortably overhead.'

'What's more, unless I'm mistaken, you had an understanding with the king of France to marry your son Alfonso to the duchess of Angoulême, right?'

'Yes, of course. Actually, that pact is still under discussion, in fact, negotiations are pretty well advanced.'

'Unfortunately I must tell you, my good sir, that your negotiations have been discontinued.'

'What are you saying? Whatever can have happened?'

'Something that is very familiar to me because these devia-
tions have long been a constant in my life: in the past few days,
all of your alliances have shifted. King Louis of France has just
signed a treaty with Spain for the partition of the Kingdom of
Naples and now he can finally march south into Italy to take
possession of his new realm. And voilà, given the fact that the
path from Paris to Naples necessarily passes through Rome,
the king requires my father's permission to cross through the
Papal State with his troops. And so, the way things now stand,
King Louis cannot afford to make the pope unhappy, which
means your hopes of marrying your firstborn son off to the
duchess of Angoulême are futile; in her place you will accept
me as your daughter-in-law.'"

At this point the duke turned to his son, who sat open-
mouthed, and in a voice rich with irony said to him: "There,
now, you're free to do all the laughing you like!"

"What, in short, she came in person to extort you and warn
you that you're hopelessly trapped, and that you have no choice
but to accept everything that the pontiff intends to do?!"

"Why, you haven't understood a thing I've said! Either
you're completely distracted or you don't know how to read
the facts. Lucrezia unveiled to me a project that was supposed
to remain secret. Which gives us a chance to resist the pope's
demands and impositions. We have an advantage. That is to
say, I have time to prepare and find, if not a way out, at least
some way of winning certain guarantees of our right to remain
the dukes of this city, and especially to maintain good relations
with the king of France and, why not, while we're at it, even
with the church. But making the pope pay for his wishes in
gold!"

The popess on probation

Alexander VI, precisely in order to prove how great was the love he felt for Lucrezia, dreamed up a full-fledged spectacle and cast his daughter in a very prestigious role. A sham performance that might easily have turned into a disaster, because its principal audience, the one that would give the show either thumbs-up or thumbs-down would be packed with bishops and cardinals, a crowd that was known to have destroyed even very powerful men with their contempt and backbiting.

The pope, on the pretext of having to spend time in southern Latium in order to resolve a thorny problem concerning certain landholdings, backed by an army that he'd be commanding in person, had decided he'd be away from Rome for almost a month. As a worthy lieutenant capable of running and managing the Vatican in his absence, Pope Alexander chose to appoint Lucrezia. A woman on the papal throne. And what's more, his own daughter. It's easy to imagine that even in a city like Rome—a metropolis inhabited by Romans, accustomed though they might be to everything that can conceivably happen in this world and even in hell—a decision of that kind could hardly help but arouse general astonishment and above all a snickering curiosity as to the outcome.

At the first session of the consistory Lucrezia had the choice of appearing in humble, unassuming clothing or else dressed as she usually was when she appeared in good society. But she settled on a third option: a highly unusual outfit, embroidered all over in glittering gold thread and adorned here and there with very valuable precious stones.

She greeted the appalled prelates and pulled a small sheaf of papers from a folder: "I have a letter." Skipping the customary ceremonial, Lucrezia, the Vicaress, as she was called, plunged right in and, addressing the array of attending cardinals, began speaking in a firm, clarion voice: "Several days ago, in Lombardy, between Lake Maggiore and Lake Como, a woman died whose name was renowned throughout the Po valley. She was not of noble birth; indeed, she came into this world as an illiterate peasant and, while still quite young, fled the home of her parents which was located in a small village called Cascina dei Poveri. As is so often the case in families on every continent, the father treated his daughter with constant violence. He'd beat her black and blue. One day the poor young woman found herself with a broken arm and a badly swollen eye. In search of proper medical treatment, the young woman set out on foot and after walking all day reached the summit of the Sacro Monte, a high hill set among the mountains of Varese. There, at the edge of a forest—as everyone in the region well knew—lived a hermit woman known for her prodigious skills as a bonesetter. At this point, perhaps, I should simply read you the rest of the letter and the tale it tells of this poor young woman," and here she held up the missive. "It is the abbess of the convent of the Monte Sacro who writes: 'The hands of the hermit and bonesetter were truly miraculous. The young woman, whose name was Giuliana, decided to spend her convalescence with the bonesetter, keeping her company. And she realized that she was living in an authentic and long-abandoned monastery. At the entrance was still the classic *rota*, or 'wheel,' for the acceptance of offerings, the kind that is built into the front wall of many if not all monasteries. That wheel, which provided food, water, and even clothing, spun incessantly.

"'One morning Giuliana was readying eggs, milk, and fresh baked bread to be put into the *rota* to feed the poor when to her surprise, as she turned the wheel a baby appeared in the donations basket. She offered the baby to the women of the village so that they could bring it up themselves, but they all had children of their own to feed and raise. The women of that valley had only two breasts apiece, and each with only a single teat. And so the monastery had an unexpected guest, who was however dearly loved by something like twenty mothers, because by now the host of women fleeing violence had grown to that number. The requests for aid grew rapidly. It is well-known that the easiest thing to find in this world is needy people, and those who come to turn the *rota* always hoped to find a donation that would help them survive. And so all those women, working together, whom the good people of the valley now called the Sisters of Good Succor, had to learn how to produce food, fabrics for blankets and clothing, as well as all the prayers and songs to say and sing to make lighter the hard work of hoeing and plowing, the milking of livestock, the rowing required when fishing on lakes and rivers. The renown of the two women who had founded the convent of Good Succor soon spread throughout the valley and all the neighboring mountains, at least in part because of the care they gave to the handicapped and the sick. But one bonesetting folk healer was not enough to keep up with the demand. And so other folk healers and everything-setters soon came along to offer help. But it is a well-known fact that when simple souls offer too much generosity and manage to break through the barriers of greed, soon swarms of *possessores* and privilege-holders of all kinds, beginning with certain grand prelates, are bound to prick up their ears and cast suspicions of heresy against anyone capable of producing such a wave of human solidarity. Luckily, it was not only the simple and the humble who rose up against that persecutory campaign but also a few bishops, with the support of men armed with power and wisdom. Thus, the convent came to receive recognition from the duly constituted authorities, beginning with Pope Sixtus IV, and it not only survived but grew even larger.

"'A few days ago, Giuliana, whom everyone called *la bona femmina*, the good woman, passed away. I don't what place in heaven was reserved for her, but I would ask you holy men of the curia of Rome to protect this memory and, above all, to allow the community of this convent to go on working in aid of those who suffer injustice, violence, and mistreatment.'"

After she was done reading, the popess stood up and stated: "We must give an immediate answer. And I exhort you to issue a special bull giving permission to the nuns of Good Succor to carry out their mission with absolute independence, as well as the right to expand their area of operation without limits or vetoes of any kind. I call for a vote."

Approval was unanimous, and the decision was even met with applause.

Present at this session of the consistory were, among others, the delegates from Ferrara. They declared themselves to be astonished at the sight of this momentary princess of the church surrounded by captivated cardinals who hung from her lips. But they were above all astonished at the way this young woman read a missive from a community of faithful women, driven by an extraordinary determination to put themselves at the service of the needy, and managed to lay out the actual duties of those high ministers. This made clear the intent of Pope Alexander VI. With this move the pontiff had managed to demonstrate the degree to which Lucrezia possessed not only an uncommon degree of charm, but also an inimitable capacity to hold the tiller of such a challenging and delicate position of governance.

Matchmaker of herself

As Lucrezia carried on her important work, she also found herself involved in the dispute with the representatives of the duke of Ferrara over certain clauses of her nuptial contract. In truth, this too was another brilliant maneuver on the part of the master of the house of Borgia, that is, the father of the bride. The fact that she herself was authorized to conduct the negotiations only elevates the weight and value of the complete independence this young lady could rightly boast. As we have seen, Duke Ercole intended to extract the greatest possible profit from that wedding, exactly as the likely bride had suggested he do. While the pope himself was strongly motivated to ensure a positive outcome to the negotiations, the duke of Ferrara's demands were nonetheless exorbitant, to say the least. Lucrezia's prospective father-in-law was demanding no less than 200,000 ducats as a dowry, plus various territories with accompanying castles, special privileges for the duke's younger sons, as well as the complete elimination of the annual tribute that the House of Este was required to pay to the pope in exchange for their right to rule the city, of course, which was one of the Vatican's feudal holdings. In these negotiations, Lucrezia's position was not that of someone haggling for her own advantage, but rather—and shamelessly—for the absolute benefit of her future father-in-law and Alfonso d'Este, the groom-to-be.

And so the pontiff, who only weighed in toward the end of the debate, found himself obliged to comply, against his own wishes and best interests, with the demands of the duke of Ferrara. But we, always prepared to see the worst in people, are entirely certain that here too there was a masterfully conducted charade set in motion by Pope Alexander VI, who played in all this the role of the reluctant profiteer forced to give in to the wishes of his daughter and her immense influence. A role that in the end got him exactly what he wanted.

Then, on September 1, 1501, at Palazzo Belfiore in Ferrara, the marriage ceremony was celebrated *ad verba*, that is, in the bride's absence; the bride was in Rome awaiting preparations for the journey that would take her to her new home in Ferrara, a city that was finally free of meddling from both her father and her unspeakable brother.

In the negotiations it was verbally accorded that the bride could not take with her Rodrigo, her baby son, just two years old, the child of her second husband Alfonso. There is no need to elaborate on how profound the mother's grief must have been.

On January 6, 1502, the procession that had come to gather up the bride and take her to Ferrara set out from the Vatican. Just then, it began to snow. Bernardo Costabili, one of the Ferrarese envoys, tells us that "His Holiness walked from one window of his palace to another so he could watch till the very last moment the sad departure of his beloved daughter."

The procession, with knights and ladies of the retinue on horseback, set out. Lucrezia too was on horseback, but she did not ride her steed in the Amazonian style, that is, sidesaddle as was common among women in those days, but instead like a man, straddling the saddle. For that reason, she wore loose Turkish-style pantaloons, like those that Muslim women wear when they travel on ponies and camels.

The bride's caravan covered the miles to Ferrara with a considerable number of stops along the way, some by night but many by day. This was to keep her from wearying herself. And so in certain cities there were layovers of as long as three days. When they reached Foligno they were welcomed by a saraband of men on horseback prancing ahead of floats depicting allegorical scenes: young women costumed as nymphs and fauns; deities such as Apollo and Dionysus; the three Graces, half-naked; and Vulcan with his wife Venus. All the characters performed and sang to the accompaniment of musicians. Acrobats performed as well, swinging from ropes that stretched from one palazzo to another across the boulevards and streets. They made it look as if they were falling from dizzying heights but every time they won bursts of applause for the dexterity with which they managed to clutch the swinging trapezes, apparently just in the nick of time, though actually exactly according to plan. The crowd looked on eagerly as the bride was voted the loveliest of all the ladies present, whereupon a young man dressed as Paris handed her the sought-after prize: a solid-gold cast apple.

The caravan climbed up into the Apennines, from the summit of which they were to descend into Romagna. When they reached the pass to cross over the range, they once again encountered snow, an entirely normal thing to find at that elevation. Luckily, at Urbino a stop was planned at the palace of the Montefeltro family, where they were greeted by Elisabetta Gonzaga. Lucrezia was astonished to find herself sitting inside an enormous fireplace along with more than fifty other people.

Toward the end of the month of January the procession reached Bologna, and from there the bride rode to the castle of Bentivoglio. After traveling the last twenty miles, she would be in Ferrara.

Lucrezia had just retired upstairs to the suite that had been given her for the night when she heard a tremendous racket coming from the castle's front gate. A horseman had spurred his mount and jumped recklessly onto the drawbridge just as it was being raised, at considerable risk of plunging into the moat. The mad masked rider, according to chroniclers of the time, then put on a series of acts and pirouettes worthy of a veritable equestrian circus, dismounting and leaping back into the saddle at a full gallop, doing handstands and then back-flips, again into the saddle. When the guards menacingly demanded his identity, he replied with something bordering on annoyance: "Why, don't you recognize the surcoat that I wear, don't you know my insignia? I'm a courier in the service of the duke of Ferrara, and I bring a missive for Milady Lucrezia! Ask the magnificent lady to come to the window, if you would!" And with these words, he caused his steed to rear up on its hind legs.

Lucrezia finally leaned out the window and shouted: "What missive could you possibly be bringing me with such a din and clatter?"

And the horseman, reining in his steed which then kneeled until it had performed a full bow before her, replied: "I myself am the missive, I am here to bestow myself entire, for you to do with as you will, my lady!"

With those words he tore off the mask and the heavy jacket with vertical stripes that designated him as a ducal messenger. And to the amazement of one and all, behold none other than Alfonso d'Este in person. Lucrezia's emotion was uncontrollable. She shouted to the groom: "*Grazie*, Alfonso! This is the most magnificent gift I could ever have received, my lord! By all means, come up to see me, if you please, on horseback if you prefer!"

Once they were left alone in the sitting room, Lucrezia bowed until one of her knees practically brushed the floor and exclaimed: "Will you permit me, my beloved husband, to embrace you and welcome you as brides are commonly allowed to do?"

"Have you lost your mind?" Alfonso replied. "Don't you know how unseemly it is to permit expressions of affection before at least one night of love has been spent together?"

There was a moment in which they both stared aghast and then both Lucrezia and her husband burst into loud laughter. Then Alfonso grabbed her around the waist, lifted her up, and planted a kiss on her lips. They sat down together for a snack. The young man wished to eat heartily because his ride and the excitement of finally being alone with Lucrezia had given him quite an appetite. Suddenly his bride changed the subject: "There's something I really wish you'd explain to me."

"Ask away, my lady."

"I'd like to know what's happened to you. To what do I owe this extraordinary metamorphosis? Until just a few hours ago

I was more than confident that you held me in the utmost and unconcealed contempt. I had been told, even by your father, that you were revolted by the very idea of taking a woman of ill repute like me as your wife. And now it's as if I had magically replaced that unworthy person whom everyone else had represented to you as little short of the devil's own daughter!"

"Don't kid yourself, I'm still convinced that you're Lucifer's natural-born daughter, but I've suddenly discovered a powerful predilection for everything that comes from hell."

"Fine, fine, I can see that you've decided to cling to your paradoxes, and I find them every bit as amusing as you do, but since you're avoiding the topic I'll tell *you* the true reason: first of all you have been impressed to see that in the nuptial negotiations I was working on you and your father's behalf."

"It's true, I admit that. And then," he went on, "there's the detail that you even made sure that the Vatican, for the next I don't even know how many years, will not be able to deprive the Este family their right to dominion over Ferrara."

"I'm happy to hear that, but it saddens me to have to realize that in the end your love for me comes only from a matter of economic interest."

"No, what really astounded me actually was the way that you were able to move and deal with the people who surrounded you."

"Are you saying that you've seen me before? But when?"

"It was several weeks ago, the very same night that you, with the pontiff your father, danced in celebration of our wedding."

"So you were there?"

"Yes. And as I usually am, I was disguised as an unusual personage."

"Which personage?"

"As a cardinal: I wore a pair of spectacles, a fake nose, and a beard, like a perfect prelate. You couldn't have possibly recognized me. I edged very close to you pretending I was conversing with one of my colleagues and I heard everything you said. I saw your lovely eyes, your harmonious gestures, and I even caught a whiff of your enchanting scent."

They talked together, they even jested together, and before they knew it more than two hours had gone by. The sun was beginning to set and Alfonso was forced to head straightaway back to Ferrara.

"Forgive me, but unfortunately I told no one that I would be coming to meet you, and I even forget to alert the servants and the palace guards. By this time they must be very worried."

"All right, I'll come downstairs with you. In any case, I'll see you again tomorrow."

As they went downstairs she took his hand and told him: "You can't imagine what joy this surprise visit of yours has brought me! I'm so happy that I feel certain I'll have a terribly hard time tonight falling back asleep."

La leçon des italiens

We are in Ferrara. What charms and surprises us about this period is that we find the most remarkable personalities of history, science, and universal art, all thriving within the context of the courts of Italy and Europe. Raphael, Ercole d'Este, Ariosto, Leonardo da Vinci, Pietro Bembo, Lucrezia herself, Copernicus, and Michelangelo, to mention just a few of them, were all working in the heart of humanism and the Renaissance. Often they knew each other, hated and loved each other, producing—in the union of their personalities and creative energies—perhaps the most exalted and matchless moment in the history of Italian culture.

In this context, Ferrara offers a panorama that was stunning to say the least. Governed, as we have seen, by one of the most enlightened dynasties in Italy, the city had recently decided to embark on a wholesale renovation. Duke Ercole, in fact, was carrying out a large-scale project that was destined to raise Ferrara toward its goal of becoming an ideal city, the dream in those years of every creative community throughout Europe. It involved literally doubling the city's size, with the addition of a second Ferrara, built by Biagio Rossetti, perhaps the greatest urban planner of the time, in accordance with the principles of rationality and equilibrium that were so typical of the Renaissance. He had conceived a city that, especially at that time, was unrecognizable to Lucrezia, who had visited Ferrara practically incognito years earlier with her new husband Giovanni Sforza. Every new-built home, bell tower, palazzo, or villa was the product of a strict architectural design. Nothing was left to chance.

The following day, when she woke in the castle of the Bentivoglio family, Lucrezia was greeted with a new surprise. She would not be traveling the rest of the way to Ferrara on horseback, but instead aboard a river craft, a *bragozzo,* following the current of the canal that connected Bologna to the river Po. This meant that at last she would be spared the discomfort and jolting of travel on horseback and would be able to enjoy, undisturbed, the magnificent landscape covered by a blanket of white snow. The light glinting off that candid mantle heightened the blue of her eyes, giving them an enchanting intensity.

Her husband noticed it to his astonishment when, after her triumphal entrance into the city, he finally was able to spend a little time alone with his bride. They rode their horses into the old castle, the Castello Vecchio, and entered the immense four-sided portico lined with monumental columns: "My God, what spectacular flashes of light from your eyes!" Alfonso exclaimed. "Where does this enchantment come from?"

And she shot back: "Oh! It's an old trick that all us witches know how to do, you did right not to clear all the snow out of the courtyard, that way I can keep on having this effect on you!"

A number of porters walked ahead of the newlyweds, carrying on their shoulders the bags and trunks brought by the lovely new tenant. To make sure they weren't disturbed, the duke had moved out of an entire floor normally reserved for him alone. When they came to the portal that led into the large bedroom, the new bride couldn't contain an *Oh!* of wonder. In the center of the room stood an enormous wooden structure with figures painted in enamel. Alfonso gestured grandly toward four servants who simultaneously hauled on four ropes, and behold, the entire construction opened up on all four sides, displaying a bed complete with drapes that in turn vanished like so many theatrical backdrops.

Lucrezia exclaimed: "And then you charge me with practicing magic! This is wonderful! And you're saying that we can sleep inside this Noah's Ark?"

"Yes indeed, it really does seem like Noah's Ark! All that's missing is the hull of the vessel. And if you pull those cords, it all closes up around us again, as in a love nest."

You can guess at the interior from looking at the exterior, and this goes both for buildings and for human beings

From that night on, the two young people spent every night together, to the enormous satisfaction of the pope and especially of the Este family, who were eagerly awaiting the birth of an heir. But however much life with her new husband filled her with joy, Lucrezia was interested in exploring the new territory that she had barely skimmed, to her astonishment, when she had taken refuge in the convent that was being rebuilt. She asked her father-in-law to let her tour the Este family's famous country residences, known as "the delights," or *le delizie*.

Ercole treated her with unimaginable courtesy. There were those in the court milieu who claimed that the duke had actually fallen head over heels for the young woman; some even claimed that he'd announced that if his son Alfonso failed to take the twenty-two-year-old Lucrezia for his wife, he'd happily marry her instead. When Ercole provided her not only with his permission but with a band of artists and historians to serve as tour guides, Lady Lucrezia spent many days traveling from one country palace to another, including the castles perched high above the waves and overlooking the islands at the mouth of the river Po.

Alfonso could hardly stand her continual absences. By now he couldn't bear to be apart from his charming young bride. One day he couldn't resist any longer and, saddling up his horse, he left at dawn to see her at the residence of Belriguardo. As he reached the farm where travelers changed horses, he stopped to have one of his horse's loose shoes tightened, and the farrier who came out to greet him immediately said: "Welcome to my forge, Your Excellency! How is your lovely wife? Is she feeling better?"

"Why would you ask me such a thing?"

"Indeed, my lord, I saw her go by here not two days ago, stretched out on a cart, hurt from a fall."

"She fell from her horse?! When? Where?"

"Just two miles from here, hadn't you heard? In any case, it was nothing serious. As you must know, we farriers know a little something about bones and certainly, from the glance I gave her, I feel sure that she has nothing broken."

"Where can I find an inn or a tavern hereabouts?"

"You needn't travel far to find one; in fact, right around the corner is a tavern that my sister runs. In fact, it was my sister who medicated her."

"And does she have linseed oil or other such swill for massages?"

"Certainly, I'd be glad to accompany you, if you like."

An hour later, they reached the castle where Lucrezia lay recuperating. Opening the door to her room, Alfonso found her fast asleep in bed. Doing his best to make no noise, He crept closer and leaned over his bride to give her a kiss. Then and there Lucrezia woke up with a moan and, when she realized what was happening, she murmured sadly: "Oh, my love, forgive me, but I can't even brush your lips."

Alfonso replied: "Don't tell me that you hit your face too!"

"Yes, I'm afraid I'm all just one giant bruise, starting with my nose, and my mouth is swollen. Can't you hear how hard it is for me to talk? Who told you I'd taken a fall?"

"The brother of the woman who medicated you."

"The farrier?"

"Yes, and he also told me that there was probably nothing seriously wrong with you."

"He may be right, but I'm all aches and pains in every inch of my body, and it even hurts to breathe or close my eyes."

Her lover lowered his head and said nothing.

At last he spoke up: "Unfortunately, there's not a doctor in this whole area who has any idea what to do for you. Do you want me to help you take off your blouse? If you trust me, I think I can help a little."

Lucrezia pulled away in fright: "I beg of you, Alfonso, it will hurt me too much if you touch me!"

"But to touch you is the only way I know of making you feel better," he replied. "I'm admired at court and in the world at large as a reckless and dangerous horseman. I've broken more bones than I needed to in spectacular falls and tumbles, and so I've learned at my own expense how to heal myself and also how to care for others who have been badly dented. I have linseed oil and other medicaments with me. I beg of you, just trust me, I promise not to hurt you."

And Lucrezia entrusted herself to his hands. He helped her remove her blouse and very gently applied the oil, starting from her shoulders. She stifled her laments but from to time implored him: "Not so hard, please! Ahhh! I can't stand it!"

"Just be strong for a few more minutes, now try rolling onto your belly."

She went on moaning with every so often a groan or a shriek but eventually her complaints subsided and Lucrezia began to breathe a little easier. Every so often she let loose again, but Alfonso whispered to her: "If you want, I can stop . . . "

"No, no, don't even think of it, I can take it, I can feel that it's making me feel better, in fact, I like it, please continue. It's starting to hurt less and less. I love you. Apply more oil . . . Yes, that's right, there too . . . God, what a wonderful thing it is to feel your hands on me! I feel as if I've escaped from hell and been ushered into purgatory. Go on, go on, I'll be in heaven before long."

The tempests of the fantastic

One of the truly uncontrollable passions that Lucrezia couldn't conceal was her love of poetry, fanciful stories, and, above all, painting. In particular, she adored stories in which what was natural became twisted into the absurd. Those were the days in which oil paintings came from Flanders, in which Bosch depicted in counterpoint moments of both tragedy and joy, such as burning villages with terrified men and women, often naked, fleeing through the flames, set face to face with the garden of earthly delights, a sort of Garden of Eden filled with festive scenes riddled with a subtle, fairy-tale eroticism.

In Ferrara, in Palazzo Schifanoia too, the walls were painted with stories of a similar theme, in which you could see allegorical floats going by, dedicated each to a season, with renowned deities, first and foremost among them Venus: all around her white rabbits, male and female, could be seen frolicking and chasing each other lustfully in pursuit of the pleasures of feverish copulation. To no less a degree did young men and women, dressed in elegant clothing, writhe and tussle, provoking each other with furtive embraces and kisses. A few of the men strove to achieve the most unconcealed fornication, rummaging rudely under the young women's skirts. Then suddenly, without warning, a great deal of the wall was covered with little children. Some of them were newborns, laughing and wailing, crawling and running, in other words, the very apotheosis of springtime. And it was there, in the presence of that painting literally bursting with vivid cheer, that Lucrezia felt herself swept with violent gusts of fever and hot flashes, her head began to spin, and she fell to the floor, luckily caught just in the nick of time by one of the ladies of the company, all of whom cried in chorus: "Jubilation! Our lady is with child!"

That night, in the Este residence, there was a grand celebration. An heir to the throne was finally about to come into the world. The happiest of them all was certainly the duke, Ercole. But almost every bit as overjoyed was Alfonso, who was being congratulated by his whole court and all his friends; among those friends, of course, there was the inevitable dirty-minded jokester with gutter allusions that made only the filthiest of guests burst out laughing. During the party, Lucrezia embraced her spouse and whispered into his ear: "I wish I could celebrate this event properly by going back with you to our first night together," and Alfonso tenderly answered her: "You'll never believe it, but I was just wishing you could give me that very same gift."

And then in unison they burst out at the top of their lungs: "Noah's Ark!"

Everyone turned to stare at the two lovers.

Never lend cannons to anyone who might turn them on you

In covering these events we had almost completely forgotten about Cesare. Had he in the meanwhile perhaps calmed his bellicose ambitions? Not by a long shot! On the very day that Lucrezia celebrated her fourth month of pregnancy, word reached Ferrara of an event that was upsetting, to say the least. Cesare, who continued to pursue his project of conquering Romagna and the surrounding areas piece by piece, had persuaded Guidobaldo da Montefeltro to hand over to him the artillery of the army of Urbino, and Borgia intended to use those weapons to attack the city of Camerino. Guidobaldo was reluctant at first, but he finally agreed in hopes of thus winning favor with the pope. But on June 20, 1502, Cesare used that artillery to attack Urbino instead. The hapless Guidobaldo only just managed to escape. Writing to Cardinal Giuliano della Rovere he commented in astonishment: "I managed to save my life, my doublet, and my shirt. I had never seen such ingratitude, nothing more than brazen piratry."

Lucrezia, appalled, had this to say: "How disgraceful! To shamelessly betray a friend who has offered you his finest weapons, only to turn them on him in anger! What kind of justification can be expected by such a bloodthirsty brigand?" But Cesare's infamy didn't end there. A few days later, the lifeless corpse of Astorre Manfredi was found floating in the Tiber. Manfredi was the seigneur of Faenza, and he had been imprisoned by Cesare in Castel Sant'Angelo after the town was captured. Everyone immediately assumed the pontiff's son was to blame for the murder.

This cascade of atrocities, along with the muggy heat hanging over the countryside around Ferrara, dangerously weakened Lucrezia's health. And so she moved into the city, to Palazzo Belfiore, in search of a more salubrious setting, but misfortune caught up with her there, as well. In mid-July a dis-astrous epidemic of fever broke out in Ferrara, and it struck down Lucrezia along with many others. The city began to fear for her life, and that was precisely when her terrible brother came to call on her, unannounced.

That night, from behind the door to Lucrezia's room, came the sound of her voice as she berated Cesare with a series of ferocious insults in fluent Valencian. No one knows what the two siblings said to each other, but the one sure fact is that this visit delivered the coup de grâce. On the night of September 5, after horrible labor pains so dolorous that at one point she actually tried to get out of bed and run away, Lucrezia deliv-ered a stillborn daughter.

The shock felt by Ercole and the rest of the city, which was just preparing for a round of joyous celebrations, was enor-mous. But Alfonso was completely unhinged. One night, as Lucrezia lay in her bed, writhing in agony, the duke's son threw open the door and without a word sat down at her bedside, looking out the window. Lucrezia, groggy with fever, could barely make out her husband's presence, and she asked him in a faint voice: "Please, give me a fresh wet towel, I feel as if I'm burning up, I can't stand it much longer."

Alfonso, without a word, picked up a rag, tossed it into a basin full of water, and then dropped it indifferently onto her forehead, so that the chilly water dripped all over her, on her shoulders and neck.

Lucrezia jerked, startled, and cried: "What are you doing? Why, what's come over you?"

Alfonso spoke not a word and sat back down.

Lucrezia insisted: "No, what's wrong with you? Why won't you answer me? Why would you treat me like this?"

Alfonso turned toward her and spoke tersely: "Nothing's wrong."

Guidobaldo da Montefeltro

"What do you mean, nothing's wrong?" Lucrezia replied in an offended tone. "And why are you being so rude to me?"

Alfonso looked at her and replied brusquely: "I said it was nothing, and it's nothing, now stop bothering me."

With a furious effort, Lucrezia pulled herself up into a sitting position. "I'll tell you what's wrong with you. You detest me because I haven't yet succeeded in giving you the son you so desire. I'm no fool: I can see that you're afraid that, without a male heir, your brothers will push you off the throne as soon as your father dies! And that's the only thing you care about!"

Then Alfonso leapt to his feet and shouted furiously: "Nothing could be further from the truth! How can you even think such a thing? And after all, you're the last person on earth who can upbraid others for their behavior!"

"Now what are you talking about?"

"You'd be better off if I kept my mouth shut, believe me!"

"No, I want you to talk to me!"

"Leave me alone, Lucrezia!"

"Now I'm telling you, once and for all, talk to me."

"All right, then, you asked for it." Alfonso came to a halt in front of her and said, with a bitter laugh: "I'd even told my father that a less suitable bride than you was impossible to find, but he was already caught in your spell, and in time I fell under it too. What a fool I was! I even took pity on you, telling myself: 'Poor Lucrezia, she has always been used as a puppet by her father, she's been subjected to every conceivable humiliation, and what's more, the gossips and backbiters go around saying that she's a monster, a poisoner, and a prostitute.' But instead it turns out that every word of it is true! Every word!"

Lucrezia broke in, overwrought: "Have you lost your mind? What are you talking about, Alfonso?"

"I have just one name for you: Pedro Calderón, or you may know him as Perotto. I'm sure that that's how you addressed him in bed!"

Lucrezia stared at him, wide-eyed, and opened her mouth to speak, but not a word came out.

Alfonso went on: "Now it's your turn, or don't you have anything else to say? Or maybe your memory is failing you now? Sure, I can just imagine that when one has a new lover every day it's hard to remember them all. But never fear, I'll refresh your memory." And with a sarcastic, despairing smile he went on: "And yet, such a strange thing, only four short years have passed! What an ugly way to go! A faithful servant of the house of Borgia, practically an intimate of the family, you might say, found floating dead in the Tiber! Whatever could he have done to deserve such harsh retribution!"

Lucrezia covered his mouth with one hand, saying: "I beg of you, I beg of you, say not another word, I swear . . . " but Alfonso threw her back on the bed and went on: "Oh no! You wanted me to speak? Well, now you'll listen, and I want to see what excuses you have the nerve to give me! Deep down, I understand you, they'd just separated you from your first husband, and you deserved to have a little fun! Still, you might have been more careful! There's nothing wrong with taking a serving boy for your pleasures, but when a child comes of it, then things become more complicated . . . So you had another faithful servant girl help you, what was her name? Ah yes, Pantasilea! And look at what a coincidence, she too was found floating in the Tiber! You really are a family of ruthless killers!"

Just like in the kind of theater that was then in vogue, at this point there is nothing left for us to do but drop the curtain and change the scene: at the Palazzo dei Diamanti, Duke Ercole was deep in discussion with his advisers.

"The raids and ravages of Duke Cesare," he was saying, "are becoming more and more worrisome. We don't know what the best approach would be in this situation."

"If the pontiff's son continues in this manner," one adviser replied, "there's a serious risk that the balance of power in Italy will be completely upset."

"It's true," said another, "but keep in mind that there is nothing we can do to interfere, given the fact that Cesare's sister is the bride of His Excellency Don Alfonso."

Just at that moment, Lucrezia walked into the council hall. Her face was white as a sheet as she glanced at the duke and murmured softly: "I beg of you, my liege, I must speak to you. If you will."

The advisers rose to their feet as one and stood aghast. They turned to gaze at Ercole who, after a brief moment of indecision, spoke to his ministers: "Gentlemen, the council meeting will resume this evening, I ask you all to withdraw."

Immediately, in a buzz of confusion, the room emptied, leaving Lucrezia and her father-in-law alone. She stepped forward, placed a hand on his shoulder, and finally sat down, heaving a deep sigh.

"What's wrong, Lucrezia?" Duke Ercole asked in a worried voice.

"My good sir," she began, "I can no longer remain in Ferrara, I must leave."

Ercole stared, incredulous, and sat down next to her, still without a word, waiting. Lucrezia went on: "Your son has acted toward me with a contempt that cannot be countenanced."

"But when did this thing happen? What are you talking about?" her father-in-law stammered.

"I'm speaking the truth. Yesterday my husband leveled a number of terrible charges against me. I said nothing in reply, I remained silent."

"But what are you saying?" Ercole asked in confusion. "Be more specific!"

"It serves no purpose for me to repeat his words, I am sure

that your informants have already reported those same insinuations to you, in the past. Yet that concerns me very little, after all, so many foul things have been alleged against me . . . "

"You cannot behave like this, Lucrezia!" Ercole broke in. "Will you explain once and for all!"

Lucrezia took both his hands in hers and began to speak: "It's about that horrible story of my supposed lover found dead in the Tiber, and a secret son that my father allegedly recognized as his own. Don't try to tell me that you've never heard these things . . ."

The duke dropped his gaze, with an almost guilty look, and Lucrezia went on: "It matters little, my lord. If you only knew for how many years I've been listening to this vicious backbiting . . ."

"But why did you not defend yourself? It almost seems as if you are confirming this horrendous gossip!"

"It wouldn't have done any good, my liege, these stories have been repeated so many times that by now it's as if they'd taken the place of the truth. And after all, your son wouldn't have believed me, as upset and brokenhearted as he is. And I can sympathize. Alfonso has done all he could to love me faithfully, he did his best to erase all the lies he was told, but the relentless drumbeat of slander never fails."

"Wait, be patient, before you make any drastic decisions. I understand that you have been offered a grave insult . . . "

"I'm not offended, I'm just very sad."

"Listen to me, my daughter, his mother died too early, and so I was forced to take her place in this as well. I've learned to read every emotion in his soul just by looking at him, and I can tell you that not only is Alfonso in love with you, he absolutely adores you. But since I also know the way he thinks, I would recommend that you treat him the way you'd treat a fine wine aging in an oak barrel: right now he's seething inside, let us wait for him to cool down. Then, you can be sure, you will find him free of any and all ferment, and he'll be as captivated by you as he ever was."

Lucrezia lay her forehead on Ercole's shoulder and wet his suit with her tears. Then, without another word, she left, murmuring: "I hope that you prove to be the teller of my fortune."

To write words of enchantment

When she got back home, the young lady gathered her maids-in-waiting together and asked them whether they would enjoy having a party one evening with readings of some of the vast number of poems that Ferrara produced on an almost daily basis. One of them, speaking boldly, suggested: "Forgive me, my lady, but what if it were the poets themselves who declaimed their own verses?"

"What a lovely idea!" Lucrezia exclaimed. "And in your opinion, what topic should be set forth for them to write their compositions?"

And another lady's maid promptly offered a suggestion: "Why, it is you, Milady Lucrezia: you'd be the finest topic imaginable!"

That very evening, at Palazzo Belfiore, a party was held with the participation of several of the finest men of letters of the city. For the occasion, Lucrezia wore a magnificent dress and a ruby in the middle of her forehead, a wedding gift from Duke Ercole. Among those addressing the attendees, particularly noteworthy were Celio Calcagnini, Niccolò da Correggio, and Antonio Tebaldeo.

Tebaldeo stood up and announced: "Milady Lucrezia, with your permission I would like to read a sonnet that Marcello Filosseno had written for you." The poet began: "*Godi Ferrara, poi che il ciel disserra / bel dono in te, che al tuo sceptro provede / locando hora Lucretia in la tua sede, / Lucretia in cui suo ben*

Natura serra." ('Rejoice, Ferrara, as the heavens open / a lovely gift to you, the source of your sceptered future / by placing Lucrezia within your walls / Lucrezia in whom Nature herself conceals her greatest good.')[4]

Lucrezia, flattered, moved among the guests, striving to put them all at their ease. Everyone found the young lady captivating. One of them tried to get to his feet, clearly with considerable difficulty, using a crutch as support; indeed, without that crutch, he evidently would have been unable to stand up. The hostess leaned over and said: "Don't worry, you need not stand up to greet me."

"But I too," the lame young man spoke up, "would like to dedicate a poem to you."

"Oh, most happily!" And with those words she helped him to his feet.

The poet immediately began to present his story: "This piece has a title, and it's *For a Smile.* Here it is: 'I am an oarsman and I push my oar along with all the other sailors so that the boat in which I work can cross the Grand Canal. One day, on that luxury craft, that Bucintoro of a galley, a merry brigade came aboard, with many lovely young ladies and young men of high lineage. The chief of the group called out loudly: "Among you is there no one who will sing us a song as we cross the canal?" "I will!" I replied, offering to sing. And so I began to sing a ballad dedicated to one of the fair ladies, by far the most dazzling. When I was done, that lady came over to me and smiled, deeply moved, then she disembarked with the other passengers and vanished. All that night and for many nights that followed that smile kept me awake. It appeared before me wherever I turned, especially when I was rowing.'"

---

[4] Various Authors, *Lucrezia Borgia. Storia e mito*, Leo S. Olschki Editore, Florence 2006.

And so saying, the speaker swept his crutch as if it were an oar and went on.

"'I'd had enough, I could no longer work on that boat. I decided to enlist as a soldier. A friend of mine was a captain and he was in Naples. I went to see him and he helped me enlist in the king's army. Just a month after that, I found myself in battle and the enemy was charging to the attack. They had already broken through the front lines of horsemen and infantry. They were charging toward the king himself, I surged into the melee and managed to strike down the first enemy soldier and kill him. "Soldier!" the king cried to me. "I owe you my life. Without you and your sword I would be dead now." And so he embraced me and said: "To me from this day forth you are like a son to me." There was another battle and I stayed close to the king's side once again. We were victorious. I had fought like a lunatic, and I had taken command in place of the captain-major when he was killed. The king named me general and I always acquitted myself honorably. In the last battle in the Po valley we captured the whole court of the king of those cities. And there I immediately recognized the lady of the smile. She was the queen. I took advantage of the confusion, I grabbed her and pulled her up onto my horse. We fled together. In one of the villas that the woman owned in the countryside, we made love all night long. The next day I went back to my army and, two days later, I learned that my queen had come to terms of peace with the enemy king, who was after all my king. They decided to marry. The kingdom would thus be safer. One night and then everything came to an end. I boarded a brigantine, bringing a great deal of money with me. I made a deal with the captain, and I bought the ship as well as command of it. But as fate would have it, we encountered a Saracen vessel. There was a great sea battle, and we were all taken prisoner, and now here I am, rowing as a galley slave. Now I push my oar to the beat of a drum pounded by an oarmaster, who also delivers snaps of a horsehide whip. As

I row, I think to myself: *But what happened, and why?* And I answer my own question: *It was all for a smile.*'"

There was a burst of applause, after which Lucrezia, as deeply moved as the smiling queen, went over to the young man and sat down next to him.

"Is this story yours? And if it is, when did you write it?"

"Why do you ask me that?"

"Because I envisioned my brother in these battles and in the end I took it as an omen. I saw him rowing, in chains."

"I don't know, perhaps. For that matter, Cesare is someone that everyone is aware of, he's a common subject of conversation. But if I may, my lady, I'd like to extend my congratulations for your decision to invite us all here this evening. In the name of one and all, I believe I can safely say that we're all honored by your gracious generosity."

Lucrezia, flattered, replied: "I thank you and I wish I could have evenings like this all the time. But help me by selecting the people who can best embellish such evenings."

"I hardly know that I will be up to the task that you ask of me."

"If you truly wish to please me, then I'd ask you to place your trust in me and be less formal with me. I will tell you that I have never needed a friend as much as I do right now. But forgive me, I don't even know your name!"

"Ah, allow me to remedy that immediately. My name is Ercole Strozzi. My occupation is Judge of the Twelve Wise Men, and like all those who serve justice, I try to escape the trap of duty by dabbling in poetry."

An invitation to a banquet to serve coffins

In the meantime Cesare, who by now was the master of Romagna, was working to expand his dominion ever further in the hope of building a full-fledged realm of his own in central Italy. His reach was broadening, extending to include Bologna, Siena, Pisa, and Lucca. But around him, inevitably, the number of men and women who wished to see him dead grew. Among them were not only his openly avowed enemies, that is, the various lords and seigneurs who were afraid of winding up like Astorre Manfredi, bobbing dead in the Tiber river, but even many of his closest supporters. In fact, Cesare's own captains were fearful of the enormous power that their chief was accumulating. As Machiavelli wrote: "These matters coming to the knowledge of the Vitelli and Orsini and their following, it appeared to them that the duke would become too powerful, and it was feared that, having seized Bologna, he would seek to destroy them in order that he might become supreme in Italy."

These men gathered at Magione, in the home of Cardinal Giovan Battista Orsini, to organize their conspiracy. But once he learned of the plot, Cesare Borgia undertook a cunning and horrifying vendetta.

He pretended that he wished to come to an understanding with his rebellious captains and he blandished them with offers of prebends and great personal advantages. After soothing their fears and suspicions, he invited them all on December 31, 1502, to a banquet in the city of Senigallia. No matter what else we might say, we must admit that this episode shows that Cesare possessed a profound familiarity with history. In fact, this tactic of inviting one's enemies together to exterminate them all was an old and infallible tactic, recounted even by Xenophon, the Greek historian, one of the few who did not take part in the banquet held by the Persians for the leaders of the Greek army, a banquet at which all the generals invited were slaughtered wholesale.

Cesare went out to welcome the former conspirators and, speaking to one of them, Vitellozzo Vitelli, he said with a smile: "Brother, how could we, who have fought together and achieved so many great conquests, ever think of disagreeing? I am willing to forgive and forget, come, give me a hug!" and he kissed him on the cheek in a sign of peace.

They all walked together into a large hall where a table groaning with rich foods awaited them—roast game and an abundance of fine wines.

"Now listen carefully," Cesare had said to the cook, "I want their last meal to be the finest meal of their lives."

And in fact, once they had all had their fill, Cesare said: "Forgive me, my friends, but I am afraid I must leave you for a moment, in the room adjoining this one there is a poor young girl who cannot stay a day without a visit from me, and for that matter, as we like to say, the finest dish you can sink your teeth into is a buxom wench!"

The captains burst into lewd laughter and Cesare left the room. Immediately thereafter a platoon of guards burst into the room, surrounding the horrified banqueters. A few of them tried to escape, but they were instantly run through. The slaughter began. Two of the conspirators were strangled that same night by Michelotto Corella, Cesare's personal assassin, who had already murdered young Alfonso of Aragon, Lucrezia's second husband. Two others, in the cruelest fashion imaginable, were held prisoners for a few days, so that they nourished hopes of salvation, only to be killed—one throttled and the other drowned.

It should be said that at the time this infamous exploit of Cesare's won more praise than outrage. What awakened the admiration of one and all was the great cunning and determination, the qualities of a true condottiere, with which he had rid himself of his rivals. Evidently certain atrocities, when they favor political or personal interests, can also be seen as positive factors. These are things that happen, or perhaps we should say, these are things that happened in the seventeenth century.

Chatting about cadavers

The scene is set in the great hall of the palazzo where Lucrezia lives, and the ladies in waiting of her retinue are preparing to welcome their guests for the evening. In fact, that night they will once again be welcoming the authors of poems and novellas and listening to them as they read their works.

Ercole Strozzi served as host in the absence of Lucrezia, who was strangely late in arriving.

"Here she is at last!" exclaimed one of her lady's maids, hurrying toward her as she entered the room.

Lucrezia, ashen-faced, crossed the room without a word to a soul. She went and sat in a chair next to the fireplace and put her hands on her face. She burst into loud tears. All the guests gathered around her.

Strozzi bent over her and asked: "Madame, what's wrong?"

Lucrezia looked up, dried her eyes with her handkerchief, and tried to reply but found she could not utter a word.

One young man politely moved the guests away, begging them: "Please, let her get some air. I heard about it on the way over here. It was inevitable that this massacre should take place."

"What massacre are you talking about? Will you tell us what's happened?"

Another of the guests answered: "What's happened is that Cesare invited all his captains to dinner in Senigallia and then ordered them slaughtered."

A voice asked: "A massacre?"

"Yes, but if the Duke of Romagna hadn't taken drastic steps and unleashed that ferocious mayhem, today we and especially Milady Lucrezia would be here mourning over him."

"Are you saying that his faithful followers were laying an ambush for him?"

And another voice piped up: "Then it was legitimate

defense! But do you have any idea of what you're talking about? Excuse me, but just who are you?"

"My name is Ariosto, the son of Niccolò."

"Ariosto? And by what right are you here?"

"By the same right as you, I would imagine."

A handsome young man who was standing close to Ercole Strozzi commented: "I'd be careful about voicing such wholesale judgments, without first knowing all the facts."

Ariosto retorted: "Well, what other information could you ask for? It's a situation that we've already come to know in the past few years. Two opposing fronts are preparing to eliminate each other, one by one, and the side that is fastest will rub out its opponents. It's an almost mathematical conclusion."

"Right," replied the handsome young man, practically laughing as he spoke. "And since mathematics is the science of the calculable and the foreseeable there's little to be astonished at. The one who slits the other's throat first wins. The important thing is not so much the contest itself but the ability to create a discussion and to prove, however ruthlessly, the power of one's own rhetoric! As if they were so many delicious pieces of fruit, the corpses of murdered men are tossed onto the table where one dines on words, maintaining all the while that these are just the ordinary facts of the times we live in, things to be accommodated and accepted as necessities. A dead man at lunch, a corpse during a horse race, an oath during the Sanctus, these days all of it's normal fare. Indeed; it's strange that here in this magnificent palace we should be *without* a coffin filled with murdered men! To say nothing of the fact that it matters little whether the lovely lady who is our hostess is living in a hurricane that is tossing her into the blackest despair. In the logic of these things, the fact that we're talking about a relative of hers should be considered nothing more than a chance mishap, to be covered with a large and heavy conversational stone."

Pietro Bembo

As the young man was giving free rein to his eloquence, Lucrezia had gotten to her feet and was walking by her young defender. For a moment she stopped, looked down at him, and asked: "Am I mistaken or are you Messer Pietro Bembo?"

"Yes, that's me, Signora."

And she said: "I thank you for your consideration of my state of despair, and I hope we shall meet again, good sir." Then she continued along, accompanied by Strozzi, who spoke to all the guests almost immediately and asked them to be understanding of the situation.

Everyone left.

Bembo was about to do the same thing, when Strozzi gestured for him to follow, and a moment later Bembo found himself in a room looking out onto a vast balcony.

The lady was at a distance, in the open air.

"Come forward, good sir, you're in the shadows and I can't see you clearly."

Bembo took a few steps and stopped in the middle of the room, not far from Lucrezia.

"Signora . . . " he began to say, but then he fell silent, staring at her in disbelief.

Lucrezia went over to him, took him by the hand with a smile, and said: "Handsome boy that you are, Raphael, put me in your portrait and hold me tight. If you don't wish to love me, sweet Raphael, mark me out of your painting, better to die if I can't belong to you."

Bembo looked at her in confusion. After a long silence he finally managed to say: "Milady, perhaps you take me for some other man . . . "

"That's true," laughed Lucrezia. "You are so similar to Raphael, the painter, that you remind me of the poem that the ladies of Rome wrote to the master. And I'll tell you that the resemblance does you no dishonor."

"Madame," said Bembo, recovering his presence of mind,

"you snatch me away from reality into a paradox outside of time and reason, and this is so sublime that I'd like to bring it back with me among my fellow men and live alone in this enchantment."

"Why, that's unbelievable . . . How easily you are able to express such uncommon images!" Lucrezia said, as if stunned. "Come back soon, and we can go on astonishing each other."

Speak of love and walk with the lame man

Ercole Strozzi, leaning on his crutch, had a hard time keeping up with Bembo, who was striding long-legged through the streets of Ferrara, blind to everything around him.

"You had told me that she was sublime, adorable! Why lie in this fashion to your good friend, my good Ercole?"

"Why do you say I'm lying?"

"Oh, please, you shouldn't have to ask! Lucrezia is so far beyond these and any other words! You took me to meet her without warning me that you were taking me to walk precariously on the tightrope of the impossible, in the presence of absolute beauty."

"I wish I had some paper with me," Strozzi joked, stopping to catch his breath, "because you're composing poems, my good Pietro, it's just too bad they're in the vernacular!"

Bembo turned and stared at his friend with a penetrating smile: "Listen to me, Ercole, learn to write in the vernacular, so that our poetry can be read by women who understand love's ways."

"I feel as if I've heard this somewhere before . . . In any case, if you say so, my friend, I'll give it a try. Because, among other things, I'm invited to a ball in Palazzo Belfiore by Milady Lucrezia."

"You are invited?" Bembo exclaimed. "And what about me?"

"From what I've been able to surmise," Strozzi murmured, "you no longer need any invitation."

To no longer feel desire would be the worst punishment of all

On the evening of the ball, the halls of Palazzo Belfiore were full to bursting with garlands and decorations, as well as elegantly garbed guests who seemed to be competing among themselves to be thought the most amiable gentleman or the most charming lady. It was January 15 and strangely the wind was gusting, so that almost as if by enchantment the sky became crystal clear and the moon managed to beam out an emerald-green light. Strozzi and Bembo were standing by a window, a certain distance from all the others.

"Will she come?" the latter of the two finally asked in a voice that bore traces of something approaching anguish.

"She invited us, after all," replied the former, laying a hand on Bembo's shoulder. "It really would be a ridiculous prank if she didn't."

As if in reply to the worries of her friend and confidante, Lucrezia, preceded by several ladies in waiting, made her entrance into the room. She was still wearing a crimson cape.

Among the comments of admiration from one and all, she stopped in the center of the room and looked around.

The instant her gaze met Bembo's, she went over to him resolutely and held out her hand, saying: "Messer Pietro, you alone, I feel certain, will be able to guess what the finest compliment I could hope to receive tonight might be."

Ercole Strozzi looked curiously first at Lucrezia and then at his friend, who slowly reached out to take the hand that the lady was offering him. Then Bembo invited her to follow him.

They reached the large window overlooking the grounds, and Bembo swung it open and said: "Look up there," and pointed at the moon. "At a window the moon has appeared, my love can see her reflection in that moon, the pale moon has come and then wrapped herself in wispy clouds."

"Oh no, now that's not fair," Lucrezia exclaimed. "How on earth will I be able to keep up with you from this moment forward?"

"Signora, do you think it's wise to expose yourself in this way to the gossip and untruths of the malicious?"

"To what are you referring?" asked Lucrezia with feigned naïveté.

"I meant to say," Bembo replied, with some confusion, "to honor so visibly just one of your guests, while ignoring all the rest . . . "

She smiled.

"So many groundless rumors have circulated about me, I certainly must have the right to start one or two that at least have a pleasurable basis in fact . . . "

"While I believe, on the other hand," he added, discreetly, "that the truly beautiful things in life take on even more value if they are kept hidden from the world."

"If that is the case," replied Lucrezia, "then tell me what you're hiding from me?"

"Milady, that would take a whole book, if I wished to tell you what you ask."

Lucrezia gripped Bembo's hand tightly and then let it drop; then she moved off to greet her other guests.

A few days later, in the garden of Strozzi's villa, the two friends saw a servant hasten toward them, bearing a folded sheet of paper sealed with red wax.

Strozzi grabbed the letter, took a quick peek inside, then handed it over to Bembo: "It's for you, and I think I may have guessed who sent it."

Bembo opened it, read the first few lines, then turned to his friend: "I already know what's in it, it's a section of a poem that Lucrezia recited to me the last time I saw her. I found it so extraordinary that I asked her to send it to me in writing."

With those words, he handed the sheet of paper to Strozzi, adding: "Do me a favor and read it to me aloud."

The other man took it but then stopped: "It's in Aragonese."

"Of course it is, it was written by Lope de Estúñiga. But read it anyway, even if you don't know what it means, I'll translate it for you as we go."

His friend started reading: "*Yo pienso si me muriese.*"

Bembo translated: "I think about if I died."

Strozzi went on: "*Y con mis males finiesse desear.*"

"And with all my sorrow I stopped desiring."

"*Tan grande amor finiesse que todo el mundo quedasse sin amar.*"

"To deny so great a love could leave the whole world without love."

"*Mas esto considerando mi tarde morir es luego tanto bueno.*"

"When I think about it, the long wait in death is all that I could ever hope for."

Strozzi gave the letter back to Bembo.

"My friend," he said, "I've never seen anyone with your luck. Do you realize what you have? By using the verse of a poet we've never heard of, Lucrezia has declared her love for you, and added that nothing but death itself can placate this desperate passion of hers!"

To fight like warriors disguised as puppets

The next scene is set in outlying parts of Ferrara beneath a *barcassa*, that is, a large shed whose roof is made of the hull of an overturned *bragozzo* fishing boat. Beneath it a full-fledged training academy has been set up, and there young warriors learn to fight on horseback and on foot, practicing ferocious thrusts, parries, and lunges. Terrible noise was the order of the day here, with shouts of encouragement that would make you think you were witnessing a bloody charge and a fight to the death. Only here horses, shields, lances, and swords were all completely fake, because they were made of wood.

Just then, a short curtain slid to one side and Lucrezia appeared, her face almost entirely hidden behind a veil. The lady stopped, nonplussed.

"What on earth is that?" she asked the master-at-arms walking at her side. "Is it some carnival ride with spinning puppets?"

"No, Milady. Inside those suits of armor made of plaited cane are truly formidable duelists."

"What about the wooden horses?"

"It is customary to use these instead of flesh and blood horses because with every lesson real steeds would run the risk of being lamed or run through. But don't let yourself be misguided by this buffoonish appearance. Those pretend horsemen are learning more with those puppet-show wars than they ever would in real combat."

Just then, a mechanical horse, pushed and pulled by ropes and cables here and there, suddenly made to rear up on its hind legs as if mad with fear, and flipped over backward, tossing the horseman, who went tumbling head over heels across the ground. Four servants ran to help the unfortunate warrior to his feet. Then they dragged him out of the *barcassa*. "What just happened?" Lucrezia exclaimed. "Is he dead?"

"No, luckily he was protected by that armor that looks like a basket. Before long, he'll be ready to climb back onto his wooden horse. Oh, here is the gentleman that you were looking for!"

"Which one, do you mean the one walking toward us covered in basketwork from head to foot?"

"Yes, that's him, the one who just unhorsed his opponent a short while ago," and with those words he bowed low to the lady and turned to go.

The self-propelled puppet came up to the lady and gently pushed her through the curtain into a storeroom filled with wooden spears, lances, and swords, closing the door behind him. Then he removed his wicker mask, revealing the face of Pietro Bembo.

"Milady!" he began to say, looking around in dismay. "What headstrong madness has prompted you to come here, alone, in broad daylight?!"

"I know, my dear Pietro, you're absolutely right, but I couldn't wait another second!"

Bembo allowed himself a smile but still felt he had to insist: "Lucrezia, you can't run the risk of being compromised like this, we are under constant surveillance, we're being spied upon at every turn, almost certainly even now . . . " and he hastily looked around. "Are you sure that no one followed you here?"

"Don't worry, I . . . "

"How can I keep from worrying? I'd be derelict in my duty toward you."

"But I wrote you, I've waited days at a time with no reply, and I didn't know what had happened!"

"Speak softly, Milady, I beg of you!"

"Why, what are you afraid of? No one can eavesdrop on us here, they just look like so many puppets from the carnival fair!"

"Wait," he interrupted her, "you just said that you'd written me, but I haven't received a letter from you in days either."

"What are you saying? I've sent you at least four. What does this mean?"

"It means that someone intercepted them, read them, and maybe even transcribed them!"

"Don't yell at me like that, if you only knew how hard I've worked to write as beautifully as you do . . . "

At those words, at the sound of that voice, Bembo could no longer restrain himself. He grabbed her by the waist and kissed her deliriously. When they broke apart she sighed and said in a faint voice: "You've repaid me a dozen times over, more than I could have hoped, I beg you, kiss me again."

Bembo certainly didn't have to be asked twice. They contented each other's desires, at length and at leisure.

"Lucrezia, I can't resist you, but we must be careful."

"Do you mean to say that I won't be able to write you again?"

"No, that's something I'd never accept, it's the only way I have of keeping you close to me always. But we must take care, tell each other everything there is to say without letting the others understand us."

"I agree. For starters, from this moment onward I will no longer be Lucrezia."

"Then what should I call you?"

"F. F."

"Why?"

"You'll understand it yourself if you think it over for a while."

But the violent fever of this passion was not the only one to sweep Bembo under. In August, upon his return from a journey, the poet caught the tertian ague, which was still claiming victims in Ferrara and its surrounding countryside. Forced to stay on bed rest and in quarantine, he had no way of reaching out to Lucrezia.

One morning the servant who was caring for Bembo heard a horse ridden up to the villa and stop. He didn't have time to get downstairs to see who it was: Lucrezia had already thrown the door wide open and was coming up the stairs.

"Milady," the servant stammered, "you can't be thinking of getting close to him . . . It's too dangerous . . . You could be infected just like him."

He hadn't finished speaking before Lucrezia opened the door to Bembo's bedroom and saw him lying in a daze in his bed. At first, he wasn't even aware of her presence.

"My love . . . Pietro, it's me."

Bembo turned and looked at her: "Forgive me, but everything is so blurry, who are you?"

"Don't strain yourself," she said, and then she held his wrist and took his pulse. After that she brought her face close to his: "God, you're on fire!"

Pietro replied, moaning: "Who are you? Don't come so close to me . . . It's dangerous . . ."

Then, suddenly: "Lucrezia! You're Lucrezia!"

"Yes, it's me."

"I recognized your perfume." Then he let her embrace him, until he suddenly cried out: "No, you can't do that, you might die too!"

Just then a woman arrived with a basin and some towels. Lucrezia said: "What is that?"

"Cold water."

"Good, good, give it here."

She took a towel and dunked it in the water. Then she laid it on his forehead, as he moaned in pain. Lucrezia felt Pietro's neck and chest with one hand and exclaimed: "But he's soaking wet!"

And the servingwoman said: "Signora, this is the ague, the tertian fever . . ."

"But you can't possibly think of leaving him drenched like this! Especially in a room as chilly as this one. Don't you have a brazier in this house?"

"Yes, it's downstairs, I'll bring it up directly."

While the servant woman pushed the brazier into the room,

Lucrezia lifted the blankets and said: "We must get these clothes off him!"

"Take his clothes off?"

"Certainly, we have to dry him. Do you want to leave him sopping wet like this? Come help me now!"

"Of course," and together they began drying him off.

Lucrezia let slip a muttered comment: "God, not even St. Sebastian can compare with you . . . There, now he really is dry."

After a while the servingwoman commented: "In any case, he'll be as wet as he was before long."

"Well, then," said Lucrezia, "we'll have to do what one does when treating a feverish child."

"What do you mean, what do children have to do with it?"

"Don't you have children of your own?"

"Yes."

"And when they have a fever, what do you do? Don't you hold them close to you to bring down the heat?"

"Yes, I do the same thing, it's true."

"Then it's up to me to calm his fever." And so saying she freed herself of her own clothing and slipped under the covers next to him. And she said to the woman: "You can go, and make sure no one comes in to wake him back up again."

Bembo moaned miserably: "I'm shaking all over . . . My God, I'm so cold . . ."

She replied: "Don't worry, you'll feel better soon, stay close to me . . . Closer, closer still . . ."

The ashen-faced woman in black always arrives but never knocks at the door

When it was summer in Rome and the heat was oppressive, it was the custom of the papal court to take refuge in the cool of the Alban Hills. But during the month of August 1503,

Alexander VI had chosen to remain in Rome, in part because the political situation, with a French army not far away fighting the Spaniards for control over the Kingdom of Naples, demanded the constant presence of his authority.

Now seventy-two years old, the pope, Rodrigo Borgia, did his best to stave off the discomfort of the heat by going to dinner one day at the home of Cardinal Adriano Castellesi di Corneto in the Colli Romani, the hills south of Rome, together with Cesare and several high prelates. They drank a toast with a chilled white wine and began to sup.

Suddenly one of the dinner guests felt faint and slid out of his chair. Pope Alexander stood up to offer him help but then he too collapsed to the floor, followed by his son who, as he fell, seized the host and tumbled with him to the floor. But the one who seemed to feel worst and who vomited in continuation was Cesare. The servants tried to help him by giving him large quantities of milk to drink. The immediate verdict was: "This was poison."

The pope and his son were immediately taken back to the Vatican. The disease that had struck the two Borgias was kept strictly secret, and the same was true for the bishops and the other noble guests. Only scattered information managed to filter out. The so-called well informed members of the curia spoke of malaria, but it was decidedly odd that a serious bout of that frightening illness should have come over those men of the cloth all at the same time, and all at the same meal.

There were others who felt certain that the tragedy that befell them was the product of a sequence of misunderstandings and errors. The poison, they said, had been meant for Cardinal Castellesi, the master of the house, but in the confusion of pouring out the wine and drinking the toasts, the full glasses had supposedly been given to the wrong people. Note carefully that this succession of pratfalls and pouring mistakes would later become a standard feature of numerous performances of the Commedia dell'Arte, where the pope and other guests were replaced by Pantaloon and other masks of the troupe of the Giocosi.

But the ironic twists and turns of a grotesque comedy don't stop here. The rumors that proliferated in the days that followed spoke of a pope on the road to recovery, but said that Cesare was already dead as a doornail. Instead, on the night of August 18, 1503, thirteen days after that fateful dinner, Alexander VI finally died after a long, drawn-out agony. As soon as Cesare, who lay in bed in a room directly above his father's, heard the news, he hurried downstairs and, at the sight of his father's lifeless body, burst into angry tears.

He soon managed to regain control of himself and shouted to his men: "Run, take away the jewels, the silver, and the money! There must be at least three hundred thousand ducats in my father's suite!"

And he was just in time because, at the very same instant, as in any self-respecting plot twist, the servants were already looting the pontiff's rooms.

No one watched over his body during the night. The next day the corpse was placed on the catafalque, but then abandoned because the guards were busy trying to steal the wax candles. Meanwhile, Rodrigo's corpse was decomposing horribly, to such an extent that the face turned completely black and the swollen tongue filled the gaping mouth. But the ferocity of the paradox reached a crescendo when it became clear that the coffin was too small to contain the body. The gilt mantle was removed to see if that helped, but when even that proved to be insufficient, the cadaver was forced into the casket with jerks, shoves, and wallops.[5]

[5] Ibid., p. 200.

No one ever has to teach children how to recognize the smell of their mother

In the midst of this cavalcade of events, Lucrezia suddenly remembered her son. This was the most painful loss, the one that had often made her feel like an unworthy woman. But her wish to go to Rome to take him in her arms had always been thwarted by the horrible customs that forbade her from displaying her motherly instincts in order to show respect for her marriage to the son of the Duke of Ferrara.

This time, however, as her whole world seemed to be collapsing under her feet, she found the strength to overcome all taboos and conventions. She made the journey, riding practically nonstop, to see her father's corpse, and especially to reach as quickly as possible her long-abandoned son.

When she got to Rome, she learned that the child was with his governess riding in the fields around the Coliseum. She went there and spotted him riding all alone on a small horse, intent on making his mount go at a trot. She rode up to him, dismounted, and stopped him.

"Ciao, lovely bambino, do you recognize me?"

The little boy looked at her for a moment, then said: "No, Signora. I'm sorry but Assunta, who takes care of me, says that I shouldn't talk to strangers."

"But, darling, I'm no stranger, I'm your mamma."

"Oh, really? Actually, they told me that you were dead . . . "

"My God, are you speaking the truth? What am I doing? I don't see the boy for two long years and he's only four, and now I expect him to come running into my arms . . . "

"I don't understand what you're saying, Signora . . . Perhaps you've mixed me up with some other little boy. Forgive me, but Assuntina has come back, I'm sure you won't mind, but I have to go now." So saying, he dug his heels into his little horse and rode off.

Choking back her tears, Lucrezia decided to go and pay her last respects to her father.

When she reached the Vatican she saw her brother, Cesare, coming down the steps to greet her, but in particular to block her: "I beg you, don't go to see him, the disease that killed him also disfigured his face. I don't want you to have such a horrible memory of our father. In fact, my advice to you is to immediately leave this city. Revolts have broken out in every part of Rome and we Borgias are looked upon as the cause of this vast ruin."

Lucrezia allowed herself to be convinced. She turned to wave farewell to her brother, but he had already vanished.

All alone, Lucrezia wandered through the rooms of the Vatican, uncertain even exactly where she was. Visions of her long-lost son and her father weighed upon her. She dropped down onto a bench near one of the palace's entrances and sat weeping silently. Suddenly she sensed a presence beside her and felt someone take her hand. She turned, startled, and found herself gazing into the face of her father-in-law, Ercole. Without a word, she threw her arms around his neck and burst into sobs.

"Thank you," she finally managed to choke out, "thank you, sir . . . Father."

"Oh!" the duke smiled. "If only I could have had a daughter like you, who knows where we would have been right now, instead of standing here weeping!"

"What you're saying is so sweet. You are the only person in the entire court to come all the way down to Rome to express your affection."

"How could I have ever thought of leaving you alone, with the fondness I feel for you . . . "

"I share something with you that was completely lacking in my relationship with my real father: trust. With a parent like you I would have always been inclined to tell the truth."

"I too know what it means to be bereft, to be left alone."

"Yes. It's a loss that we both share. My husband leaves every year for long months, and he goes to the north so that his infrequent letters only reach me long after he's returned."

"I ask myself, why does he always have to travel so much, what does he lack in Ferrara, his hometown? He says that I'm sending him abroad to learn the art and science of combat, but it isn't true . . . "

"Do you know what I think?"

"No, what?"

"That in truth my husband cannot stand living with us."

"But why? In Ferrara he has everything that he could need, to say nothing of the company of remarkably talented men and even women, skilled in all the arts and sciences."

"But that's exactly what he can't stand! To be surrounded by brilliant minds, thoughts that are too vast, impossibly geometric buildings, and people who base all of society's values on sheer knowledge."

"Well, I don't see how anyone could prefer culverins and mortars to all that!"

"Mortars?"

"Certainly, you must know that he's practically a fanatic in his obsession with this art, he's even designed cannons himself!"

"Yes, he has tried to speak to me of these interests of his, but I can't stand to hear of them."

"Just the thought that when I die Alfonso will become the duke of Ferrara! How is he preparing himself to take care of this city? By developing water projects to grow the wealth of trade and the fields, or with medicines to better the health of his subjects? No, he is only learning the ways of war, which is to say, the art of destruction! I remember asking him one day: 'What would you rather have this city become? Athens or Sparta?'

And he replied: 'Without a doubt, Sparta!'

'Sparta? Would you like to go see Sparta someday?'

'Oh, yes!'

'Well, try all you like, but you'll never find a single stone of the city of Sparta, it no longer exists, no one even knows where it was!'"

"And then what did he say to you?"

"He said nothing for a little while, and then he burst out angrily: 'Well, better to be alive while you're alive than to be handsome when you're dead!' and he turned on his heel and left."

"Nice, what a stirring response! He should join forces with my brother, Cesare, just think what a partnership that would be: eternal glory and plenty of business for the undertakers!"

Ercole said: "You know . . . I've heard talk of your court of poets, of your . . . doings with those literati . . . ."

Lucrezia stiffened and stared at him in concern. The duke noticed and hastily clarified: "No, please, don't think that . . . I meant it in no way as a reproof . . . Indeed, I understand you perfectly . . . It is impossible to live without words and thoughts. A woman like you, who studied Greek as a little girl and read Latin easily and knew not only the palazzi of Rome but also that city's history and the artworks that adorned it, needs a steady diet of beauty above all."

"Thank you. You speak the truth. I have many books with me and I'm always looking around for others. Reading gives me great satisfaction, but I need to converse about what I'm thinking the way I need air to breathe, and I am constantly assailed by doubts about every topic, concerning new discoveries, languages, and, most of all, God. I've always lived surrounded by bishops, priests, and cardinals, and even with a pope, and I will tell you that the comfort of prayer is not enough to stave off a sense of despair. A new idea expressed aloud by learned women and men often frees me as if by magic from what we call, in our language, *sciacron*, that is, a hopeless sense of grief."

PART TWO

Pope Julius II

*Reaching the end of your life isn't enough to ensure you
get smarter*

Cesare had narrowly escaped death, whether it was from disease or poison, but that was fortune's last gift to the Borgias. Often the blindfolded goddess has fun mocking the defeated, dangling one last opportunity for a comeback before their eyes.

In fact, about a month after Alexander VI's death, Francesco Todeschini Piccolomini was elected pope with the name of Pius III, and the new pope confirmed Cesare in the rank of captain general of the church and gonfalonier. Unfortunately, the pontiff barely had time to commission Pinturicchio to decorate the Piccolomini Library in the cathedral of Siena before an ulcer in one leg took him down into the grave after a reign that lasted only twenty-six days.

The name that emerged from the conclave that followed couldn't have been worse for Cesare. In fact, after spending the past eleven years in fruitless opposition to Pope Alexander, the Borgias' bitterest enemy finally ascended to the throne of St. Peter: Giuliano della Rovere, Pope Julius II. The new pontiff instantly canceled all privileges given to Cesare by his predecessor. As in the Milanese game of *tombola*, for the last of the Borgias the tile that came out of the bettors' urn read "*minga*," which is a concise term in dialect to indicate that you've lost not only your shirt but your britches. Cesare, who had supported the election of the new pontiff in hopes of winning his favor, tried to broker a compromise that would allow him to hold on to at least a part of his possessions, by giving up some of his castles in Romagna, but the situation rapidly deteriorated.

Without the powerful backing of his father, Cesare's plans for conquest, his dominion in Romagna, even his very life were all now endangered. Julius II—after suffering a violent provocation on the part of a number of chatelains who remained loyal to Cesare and had hanged the papal envoy come to demand their surrender—decided to put an end to the waiting game. By now Cesare was simply a political annoyance, and therefore had to be eliminated. And so, with the support of the Venetians who were eager for a share of the booty, he proclaimed a crusade of reconquest.

Cesare did his best to keep his footing and to prop up the structure that was collapsing around him. First he made an alliance with the Spaniards, then with the French, and all the while revolts were breaking out in Romagna aimed at driving him out and putting the old seigneurs back on their thrones.

Lucrezia (no one would ever have suspected that there was such a fiery spirit in her) did what she could to raise troops in a last-ditch attempt to save her brother from total ruin, though anyone else would have expected the bride of Alfonso d'Este to think only of herself.

Suddenly the pope's daughter was almost completely alone, and even though she was still the wife of the duke-to-be, her position was clearly growing increasingly precarious. There was no one close to her but Ercole Strozzi and Pietro Bembo. Bembo, in fact, immediately rushed to her side to comfort her, but as soon as he saw her, in the dark, at the far end of that bedroom, literally ravaged by grief, he lacked the strength to say or do anything, and he decided that it was best to go back where he had come from.

But as he was descending the stairs he suddenly came to a halt and whispered to himself: "What in God's name am I doing?! I'm behaving like a court jester. As soon as things go sideways with some sign of impending danger I put on the dark cape and pull the hood down over my face, and turn and make haste away from trouble."

So he turned around and went galloping back up the monumental staircase. He walked back into the bedroom and came to a stop right in front of Lucrezia, who then and there stood up, astonished, and threw her arms around him, saying, "I was afraid I'd never see you again."

"Truth be told, just a short while ago, when I saw you sitting on this bed, I lost the power of speech and the courage it would have taken to come and comfort you."

And as she caressed his face she replied: "It wasn't so much your words I was missing, it was your presence."

"I really do wish that my presence was enough to wipe away all of your grief and sorrow."

"Hold me tight, I beg of you, who do I have left if not you?"

"Who do you have left? You have yourself, Lucrezia! I've never seen the kind of courage that you possess! You don't even see it. I mean, at a time like this, when everything seems to be falling in on you, you manage to spare a thought for other people!"

"What? What do you mean?"

Bembo smiled at her: "Don't worry, I'd never give you away."

"Are you trying to tell me that you know?"

"Yes, and in fact, as soon as I learned of it, my love and admiration for you exploded. I still can't believe it . . . Your brother has poisoned your life with his atrocities, he ordered the murder of the man you loved, and now that he's in danger of being swept under, instead of abandoning him to his fate, what do you do? You put together an army and pay for it out of your own pocket and send it to his assistance!"

"Please, please," she whispered, "keep your voice down! If anyone knew you were here, I'd be ruined too!"

"Forgive me, you're right, but what you did was so fine, so impetuous!"

"But who told you?"

"Can't you guess?"

"No, I swore everyone to the strictest secrecy."

"The master-at-arms who accompanied you to see me that day at the fighting academy told me about it. I had confided my fears to him, I'd asked him for advice about what could be done, and he smiled at me and said: 'Don't worry, she's already taking care of it.'"

"Yes," Lucrezia nodded, "the master-at-arms is proving to be very helpful, he's put me in touch with the mercenaries, but for the moment this absolutely must remain secret! So far we've enlisted, just think, a thousand foot soldiers and five hundred archers, but we still lack the cavalry . . . "

Bembo interrupted her: "Cavalry . . . but can you hear yourself, the way you speak? You sound like a soldier of fortune organizing an army! You're extraordinary, Lucrezia, your life is a shining example, a great and lasting lesson for me! You're . . . you're . . . ." And he finally just lifted her into the air and kissed her.

She took a deep breath and said: "But if I'm so extraordinary then why have you let so much time elapse lately between one meeting and another?"

"You're right, but it's getting harder and harder to find the opportunity . . . And now that Duke Ercole has come back . . . And my father is constantly summoning me back to Venice . . . "

"All right, all right," Lucrezia broke in. "It doesn't matter, let's just enjoy what little time is available to us. We knew this wasn't going to be easy . . . Deep down, that coarse brute of a husband of mine has a point: better to be alive while you're alive!"

À la guerre comme à la guerre

The war took place, and so did the individual battles. One of them involved an attack on the castles still held by Borgia's followers. We should keep in mind that the Venetian army was one of the most feared forces in the land, fielded by the most powerful of Italian cities. And yet the mercenary forces assembled by Lucrezia and commanded by Pedro Ramirez managed to defeat the attacking troops. No one would have chanced a penny on the odds of victory of that cobbled-together group of soldiers. And, even more unlikely, Julius II, through his representatives to the court of Ferrara, complained, practically assaulting the duke: "Does this strike you as the work of a loyal subject, my lord? To personally provide support and money to finance an army to be unleashed against the Holy Father and his allies? And all this just to pursue a policy against the church, which is simply laying claim to its own legitimate rights to these lands? Never forget that you too owe feudal ties of obedience to Rome."

And the duke replied: "And that is why I, a humble feudatory, take great care not to stray into defending the interests of Cesare and his sister, as you claim. I never gave them a center for all this, I assure you! My daughter-in-law on her own has the resources and talent to organize whatever she wants!"

But it was inevitable that events should conspire to undermine even this generous undertaking of Lucrezia's. In the face of Cesare's refusal to give up all his possessions, Julius II finally lost patience and on December 20 had him arrested and confined in the Borgia tower. That's right, the very same tower where Lucrezia had once lived and where her young husband had been murdered.

Cesare strode back and forth, pacing out the narrow space in which, after winning so many successful battles, he now found himself confined.

"Borgia!" called out one of the guards patrolling the corridor outside his cell. "There's a visitor for you!"

A hail of steel bolts screeched as the door was unlocked, and then there appeared the last person that Cesare could ever have expected to see.

"Greetings, good sir," murmured Bembo. "I'm sorry to see you given such shoddy treatment."

"Excuse me, but aren't you that Bembo, the poet who's a friend of my sister?"

"I am."

"And how did you ever get permission to come see me?"

"I'm in Rome on behalf of my father, who is undertaking a mission for the Venetian Republic. The pontiff's secretary interceded on my behalf and secured this visit for me."

"I imagine that you've come to bring me greetings from Lucrezia."

"No, Lucrezia doesn't know I'm here. But on my way back to Venice I'll stop briefly to see her in Ferrara, and I'd like to be able to give her good news about you. Indeed, I hope to be able to bring her the news that you're about to regain your freedom."

"I'm afraid that that is news you won't be able to take back to her."

"Well, personally, through my friendships in the Vatican, I might be able to arrange your release. It would all depend on whether you'd be willing to hand your fortresses over to the pope."

"Have you gone mad? The only card I have left is those castles!"

"Exactly, and this is the time to play that card. Most important of all, keep in mind how difficult it is for you, as a prisoner, and especially in this place that is so dark and dreary for you, to carry on a negotiation with the pope. Once you've been released, matters could shift to your advantage, but for now you're only endangering your neck."

"But why on earth would you do all this? From what I had heard before I was arrested, it's not as if . . . how to put this . . . Not as if your relationship with Lucrezia was going great guns . . . "

"No, it's true, the powder seems to be damp, but I am still deeply fond of your sister. She's an extraordinary woman. Are you aware of what she has managed to do to defend the lands that remain in your possession?"

"No, all I had heard was reports that she was actively working to enlist new troops."

"Well, the army that she raised has been sent into the field and it has managed to defeat the Venetian army, reinforced by contingents of the pontiff's troops, successfully keeping Cesena and Imola free."

"My sister accomplished such a thing?!"

"Yes. But this isn't the only reason that I respect her. It's a rare thing to meet a woman who always thinks of others before she considers her own interests. But tell me something, what would your plans be once you manage to regain your freedom?"

"Well, the first thing I'd do is leave Rome, a place I just can't stand anymore, especially with this pope . . . I'd head straight for Naples."

"Why Naples?"

"Because Naples is now full of Spaniards, and they're my people. And from there I could begin the reconquest of my dominions."

"All right then, are we agreed? Will you do the things I suggest?"

"Certainly, you've brought me around, it's the only way to do it."

"I'm glad to hear it, but be careful, don't put your full trust in him, because as we say in the Po valley, a contract with the pope is like a memorandum of understanding with a *papòn*, and you understand what I mean, don't you?"

And so, as expected, Cesare Borgia was released. As soon as he was able to lay hands on a horse, he galloped off to Naples. But there, precisely what Bembo had warned of in fact happened. The ambush laid by Julius II, with the complicity of those very same Spaniards from whom Cesare hoped to receive help, snapped shut like a bear trap. He was chained up and shipped straight back to Spain, a prisoner of the Aragonese.

The curtain, when it is drawn, is still not enough to dry the tears

In the meantime, back in Ferrara Lucrezia felt increasingly alone. Alfonso was traveling throughout Europe, visiting all the various courts, Bembo had left, and, worst of all, her father-in-law Ercole lay helpless in his sickbed.

It was in this climate of uncertainty that Lucrezia received a letter addressed to F. F., inviting her to a meeting, that night, outside the city walls.

At the hour agreed upon, the young woman was there, waiting, a little beside herself with fear. Almost immediately a figure approached her.

"Pietro!" she whispered, and they threw their arms around each other.

"Forgive me if I made you come all the way out here, but it was the only way to see you without running serious risks."

"How I missed you, Pietro of mine!"

"We don't have much time," he began. "I have some news for you."

"News?" Lucrezia murmured in concern.

"Yes, good news."

"Oh, please, at last! What's the news?"

"Your brother has been released from prison. He had to

give up his castles in Romagna in exchange, but the important thing was to get him out of the pope's clutches."

Lucrezia threw her arms around his neck and showered kisses onto his face, then said: "Oh, *grazie, grazie*! Behind this miracle I can sense some maneuver or other on your part!"

"In part, yes, but I beg of you, allow me to finish what I have to say, or I'll never be able to get out another word, overwhelmed as I am, it's wonderful to be swept away by you, let me tell you."

"The same goes for me, but tell me: where is Cesare going now?"

"To Naples, and I'm very worried about his safety."

"Why? I assume he has a safe-conduct pass from the pope."

"Certainly, but forgive me for what I'm about to say: no one knows better than you how little value should be attached to the promises of a pope. In Venice the saying goes: 'A good Christian never swears his loyalty on the books of the Gospel,' so just imagine how it is with Julius II, who hates your whole family! But we're talking in the open here, right behind us there's a deep recess in the rock wall, let's go there, we'll be safer."

The two lovers went to hide in that refuge, where they sat on a comfortable bench.

As he embraced her, Bembo said: "If only time could stop here and now. I dreamed that the moon had vanished from her orbit and disappeared from the firmament."

"And what would that mean?"

"The ancients used to say that if such a thing were ever to happen, then a man who fell from a high tower would just float, hovering in midair, a child tossed playfully into the air by its mother would carry that same mother aloft with it, and two lovers embracing would dissolve into each other, becoming one single entity."

"This image is splendid, though it's also absurd."

"Unfortunately, it truly is. Perhaps what is happening is that what we call my crystal—that is, my heart—is breaking. It's very unlikely that we can ever hope to meet again."

"Why so unlikely?"

"You know perfectly well. I've learned from you to gauge the situation of those I love even more accurately than my own, and right now you are in a very dangerous one. Your father-in-law is not well; his son, your husband, is on his way home; and you, I can easily guess, will soon be spending all your time by the duke's sickbed, never able to stray, because the old man deserves all the love that you willingly give him. How could you think of risking a scandal at a time like this? It would be a senseless, criminal act. You already have a life sketched out on the palm of your hand, while I am moving in quite another direction. Just remember that I have loved you to the brink of madness, and I shall continue to do so."

In spite of the precarious political situation, by now Lucrezia had managed to win the admiration and love of both the populace and the court. Her charm and her propensity to listen and come to the aid of the people who reached out to her had prevailed over all the prejudices and backbiting associated with her name, and in fact her good qualities had become renowned beyond the confines of the duchy of Ferrara.

And practically by accident, for the first time since her wedding, Lucrezia had an opportunity to meet Isabella, her sister-in-law and the daughter of the dying duke.

Out of enmity between women, sometimes a great friendship can spring

It was in order to be at her father's bedside that the Marchesa of Mantua had returned to her hometown. The two women met without any of the usual retinue of courtiers. More than actually hugging, they sketched out a stylized embrace, brushing cheeks to give the appearance of a kiss. Then they looked at each other and couldn't help but burst out laughing at this pantomime they had just put on.

"Luckily, my dear Lucrezia, you never heard what I muttered under my breath the day that you arrived in Ferrara to marry my brother . . . "

"Whatever did you say, Isabella, what curses escaped your lips?"

"Well, you see, to my eyes you were a woman with a bit of a reputation who was coming to get a buff and a polish by marrying the heir to a venerable and prestigious dukely title; a crafty lady who had dared to steal from me the home where I grew up—my mother's home."

"So you're saying that you too saw me as a man-eater on the prowl, a brazen woman out for whatever she could get."

"I have to admit that's indeed how things stood."

"Well, the fact that you've come to see me today might suggest that I've managed to change your mind . . . "

"Certainly!" laughed Isabella. "What brought me around was the clear understanding that you look upon my father not with opportunism, but with respect and an authentic love."

"That's true. For his part he has always shown me the same genuine affection."

"It's a fine thing to know that my father Ercole, who has always lived up to the name that his parents bestowed on him at birth, has two women who love him dearly at this hard moment. Unfortunately, it's not enough to make up for the absence of his son Alfonso, and my husband, Francesco."

"I'm sorry that they're not here now too. And to think that I believed that I'd eliminated all the gossip and wiped out the horrible portrait of me that so many people had concocted. There was a furious quarrel in which Alfonso hurled unforgivable insults at me. I turned to your father in desperation, and

Isabella d'Este

he reassured me that my husband, whose character he knew very well, would soon feel less rancor towards me. But what happened the last time he returned to Ferrara? I only had time to catch a glimpse of him from a distance, on horseback, before he set out again on his travels."

"The same thing happens to me, from time to time. It's strange, isn't it? Just think what fate had in mind for the two of us, Lucrezia, both married to soldiers. If nothing else, every so often my brother relaxes enough to play the viola."

"He could have become a first-rate musician."

"True, but the only music he really loves is the thunder of murderous cannons and the same holds true for Francesco."

"Don't forget about hunting," added Lucrezia.

"Right, when they can't kill their fellow man, our men console themselves by slaughtering animals."

"To love beauty is a terrible thing, if those who live alongside us refuse to even see it."

"I don't know if you're aware of this, but after his first military successes I persuaded Francesco to commission one of the most famous living artists in Mantua, Andrea Mantegna, to do a series of gigantic paintings of the Triumph of Caesar, with an unmistakable allusion to his own triumph. Well, enthusiastic about the idea of seeing himself acclaimed in such a majestic work of art, he agreed. I followed the execution of that painting closely, and I was astonished at the brilliance and the cunning of that artist's work; in particular I urged Mantegna to focus in the midst of all the glory and rejoicing on the true aim of all victorious warriors, that is, to sack and plunder the defeated city, carrying off like a gang of thieves trays full of gold, valuable statues, and the occasional woman, just for the thrill of it. And he, the chief individual exalted in that artwork, barely deigned to give it a glance, and never really seemed to realize what it was he was looking at. Worst of all, for the past two years now, he has refused to give the painter so much as a thin coin, even though Mantegna goes on working for him."

"Right," Lucrezia commented. "Art is useless to them."

"In fact," said Isabella, "when they say that they're interested it's only for one reason: to prove that they're genuine aristocrats who appreciate fine art and culture!"

"I'll confess that there are times when I hold my husband in the utmost contempt."

"As do I. How could I not? For us women, it is ever thus. I'm always reminded of Phaedra, and the way she fell in love with Hippolytus in the tragedy of that name by Euripides—Hippolytus was a man who held women in contempt and cared only for hunting."

"Indeed, there is a certain resemblance," Lucrezia said with a bitter smile.

"And do you know how the Greek tragedy ends?" Isabella asked.

"No, please tell me."

"When Phaedra discovers that Hippolytus doesn't love her, she decides to kill herself."

"And you," Lucrezia asked thoughtfully after a short pause, "are you thinking of killing yourself?"

Isabella, smiling in turn, replied: "You know, I think I'll wait a little while for that. After all, my husband does come home from hunting every now and then."

Free the prisoners

Ercole d'Este assigned a very delicate task to Lucrezia, examining the supplications and requests that reached the court, imploring aid and intercession. Why on earth that particular responsibility? Women were normally entrusted with the care and supervision of the gardens, the upholstery and window dressings in the parlors and drawing rooms, at the very most selecting the cooks and the menus for the kitchen. They would never be given the job of supervising trials and their verdicts. What could possibly have led the duke to make such a decision?

Evidently it was the discovery that his daughter-in-law possessed the talent and grit to put together an army all on her own and turn the final battle into a victory.

Many of the entreaties that Lucrezia received had to do with the release of men from the prisons of Mantua, but there were many others that came from numerous cities both in Italy and across Europe. Lucrezia had already made the acquaintance of Francesco Gonzaga in 1496, when the marquis, winner of the battle of Fornovo, came through Rome. In 1502 they began to correspond occasionally.

In one of these letters, Lucrezia requested the liberation of a poor cobbler who was accused of having stolen a loaf of bread from a priest. It was a misdemeanor and so Francesco gladly agreed to his lovely sister-in-law's request; in the concluding part of his letter, however, he wrote: "Yesterday the prisoner for whom Your Ladyship so graciously asked clemency was released. But I, too, humbly have a request to beg of Your Ladyship. She too, in fact, holds prisoner a poor soul who is as dear to me as if he were myself, and he seeks mercy of you."

A few days later a problem arose that was far more serious and knottier by far. This time it was a murder. Since the relatives of the condemned man, who came from Ferrara, believed the verdict to be unjust, they appealed to Lucrezia in hopes of obtaining justice. Here were the facts of the matter: a mechanic who worked on the locks of the river Mincio, in Mantua, was sentenced for the murder of a coworker, for frivolous motives, basically a crime among drunks.

Lucrezia, with the assistance of a lawyer she had on retainer, examined the documents from the investigation and the trial, and clearly found a number of glaring inconsistencies, vague testimony, and an absolute lack of solid evidence. And so, even though she could have demanded a careful examination of the facts directly by her brother-in-law, instead she acted independently, ordering a reexploration of the murder by her own investigators. Those investigators, who went to Mantua and stayed for quite a while, succeeded in reconstructing the facts of the case and they found that actually those very likely guilty of the murder and those who ordered it were very different individuals from the poor wretch convicted of the crime, and that in all likelihood the victim had been killed because he was interfering in a romantic relationship between his daughter and an important personage in that city.

At this point, Lucrezia wrote to Francesco and urged him to conduct a judicial review of the facts. Unfortunately days and days went by without any answer from Francesco. Lucrezia, indignant, wrote him a fairly brusque follow-up note, reminding him that the matter in question was the death sentence of a man who was probably innocent. Finally, the marquis of Mantua took action, and with surprising speed actually sent the three investigators who had carried out the investigation to meet with the prosecutors in Ferrara who had first established that there had been a crime. Both Francesco and Lucrezia were present at those sessions, and she displayed in that context a truly impressive administrative competence.

In short order, the truth surfaced. The poor wretch who was about to be taken to a scaffold and executed was nothing more than a handy scapegoat. The real murderer proved to be Alberto da Castellucchio, a Mantuan nobleman, who had decided to kill the father of a young woman he had seduced because the man was threatening to report him. In order to deflect suspicions, the powerful lord had not hesitated to bribe and threaten the judges to persuade them to sentence in his place a friend of the victim, a poor and defenseless man, in the certainty that no one was likely to come to his aid. Francesco Gonzaga ordered the condemned man to be released immediately and informed his sister-in-law of his verdict in a letter. Lucrezia was radiant with joy, and spurred by happiness she decided to travel immediately to Mantua in person to offer her consolations to the poor man and conduct him back to Ferrara to be with his family. When Isabella was informed of her travel plans, she suggested that her friend come and stay in her palace, saying that she would be delighted to have Lucrezia stay with her.

Lucrezia and the marquis brought the released prisoner back to Ferrara, where the populace greeted him with great celebrations. Francesco was quite impressed by the reception and that same evening he went to the country home of Poggio Rusco, where he had invited Lucrezia to come visit the following day. Next morning, as he saw her arrive, he leapt onto his horse and rode out to meet her. Moments later they were walking side by side up the lane that led to the castle.

"You have a fine character, my dear sister-in-law," Francesco commented. "At first I thought that you were just being stubborn because you wanted at all costs to be right."

"That was the only reason, in fact," Lucrezia laughed. "And in the end I got my way!"

"Yes, but you made me sweat like a pig with all those lawyers and those stacks of dusty documents, so you owe me some form of recompense!"

"But what on earth could you possibly want? Aren't you happy to have avoided sending an innocent man to the headman's block?"

"Is the only thing you care about helping poor wretches, or do you occasionally do something for yourself?"

"I do what I do, and I let the others talk about it."

"I don't much care for time wasted talking either, so I'll tell

Francesco Gonzaga

you that tomorrow you'll come hunting with me, which means I can oblige you to witness the execution of a number of our completely innocent feathered friends, and I will warn you from the outset that my falcon runs no risk of prison. In fact, quite the contrary, you will even pet its head as a reward."

"Just pet its head?" asked Lucrezia. "That seems like a very poor reward for a noble falcon!"

"Why, that depends, my dear sister-in-law, it depends on who's doing the petting."

The next morning the sun had not yet risen when Lucrezia rode out with Francesco Gonzaga, and his retinue of courtiers and hunters, and into the forest.

"Do you know that this is the first time I've ever gone hunting?" Lucrezia said to her brother-in-law.

"What?" he exclaimed. "That good man your husband has never taken you? What's the matter, doesn't he know how to put his boots on all by himself?"

"Is that how you speak of your wife's brother?" Lucrezia asked with a hint of resentment.

"Certainly not, that's how I speak of one who has a wife like you but has never once taken her into the woods to show her that her husband is a real man."

"Perhaps there's more than one way to prove that, don't you think?"

"How you move quickly, sister-in-law of mine; don't you think we know each other too little to speak of such things?" And with those words, Francesco took the hood off his powerful falcon, which flew straight up into the air.

The brother-in-law and sister-in-law silently tracked the bird of prey's trajectory through the sky as it circled repeatedly and then suddenly plunged into a dive and seized a hapless duck, clutching it tight in its talons. Then, as was standard procedure, the falcon flew another circle through the air, then it tossed its stricken prey toward the falconer. When he saw the big bird come pinwheeling in their direction, he gave his companion a sharp shove, ostensibly to keep her from being hit by the tumbling duck.

She let out a shriek: "What do you think you're doing?"

He grabbed her around the waist before she could fall to the ground.

"Let go of me!" she ordered.

"Forgive me if I don't comply, but if I let go of you you'll fall straight into the mud. If you really do want to tumble onto the ground, by all means, let me just move you, there's dry land over here to the left."

Lucrezia regained her composure, though she was still annoyed and embarrassed: "I'm sorry, I'm made a little distraught by this hunting."

"Why don't you take a seat here?" Francesco replied. With those words he pointed to a fallen tree lying on the ground. With his glove he was already brushing off the dirt and dry leaves. A moment later, the two of them were sitting side by side. He smiled at her and Lucrezia could hardly keep herself from responding in kind.

"You must have thought me quite clumsy, eh? A demanding young lady, and quite full of herself."

"In truth, it was I who put you in this situation. I want to confess that there was no real danger of the duck ever hitting you. That was an invention all my own."

"Really? What a scoundrel!"

"I did it to break the sense of unease that you provoke in me."

"I do?"

"You see," he replied, "when you wrote and asked me to review that poor wretch's trial and death sentence, I thought to myself—excuse me if I'm harsh—that it was nothing more than a pretext to enter into contact with me in an attempt to seduce me."

"Oh, really!"

"Yes. And it made me feel quite satisfied with myself: look at how I've captivated her! I never miss a trick! But then you wrote me another letter not much later that was practically hot to the touch, not with love but with scorching insults, an attack on my moral turpitude and lack of respect for the weak and the powerless."

"And you deserved it!"

"Perhaps I did, but the fact remains that the letter knocked me off my perch. And so I said to myself, 'Pathetic imbecile! This woman isn't playing around, she's not pretending to be a good Samaritan as a way of getting her hands on the reins of power.' Then when we met to resolve the problem with judges and lawyers, and I had a chance to witness the grit and the almost mystical seriousness with which you threw yourself into this matter in order to save an innocent man from execution, I was reminded of something that my mother, Margaret of Bavaria, the German, as they used to call her, always said: 'Judge a man or a woman by what they are able to do for others, not for what they claim to do in hollow words.'"

"In that case, why did you invite me to come on this hunting party? Perhaps you wished to rehabilitate yourself and drag me into your realm of amorous conquests?"

"No, that was certainly the atmosphere, but I had quite another objective in mind."

"And what was that?"

"To put myself before you, completely stripped of any masquerade, no mask on my face, no armor over my heart. And even though this may strike you as absurd, I've come here today to tell you that I love you."

Lucrezia, as if to conceal how this speech had moved her, commented: "Look at that, a plot twist!"

"Not really, and in fact given the enormous respect that I now feel for your person, I would never try to tempt you to make love with me. And do you know why? Because to do so would be an infamous crime. I have syphilis."

"Syphilis? And you come to tell me about it like that, as if you had the common cold? 'You know, I'm just a bit under the weather, it must have been a draft, but I'll get over it . . . ' Heavens above: the French pox!"

"Yes, it's true, I've been rather brutal, but I had to tell you so that you'd understand the depth of my despair."

"I understand but . . . Should I believe you? It seems impossible . . . I've never known anyone before who was afflicted with this disease, but I've heard about it . . . The victims can scarcely move, they lose their memory, they faint suddenly, they fall to the ground and no longer even know who they are . . . While you . . . If I were asked to imagine a healthy person, I'd imagine you. And then there's the fact that you had all those children with your wife . . . "

"True, and they were all born healthy and they've all grown up safe and sound."

"But were the two of you aware that you were exposing yourselves to such a terrible risk? Those children could have been born infected, sentenced to a life that you could hardly really call a life at all."

"Certainly, this is what I feel guiltiest about. But with reference to your doubt that I might be lying to you, I want to tell you that the disease from which I suffer is also called the *strabacco*, which means that it comes and goes: one day you're hale and healthy like a bright sun, and the next you're little more than a shadow of your former self. The day we went with the man's relatives and friends to welcome that poor wretch upon his release, and then again at the moment when we reached Ferrara to deliver him home, when I looked out at all those people cheering joyfully, I asked myself: Who are they cheering for, the innocent man freed from prison? No, it's Lucrezia, that's who they admire and love. And that was when I felt the ground give way beneath my feet. Do I have the courage, I thought, to consider taking her without any concern about infecting her with a loathsome disease? And that then she, without realizing it, would do the same thing to her husband? Why, where is my conscience, tucked away between my buttocks? I'm willing to run the risk of destroying a town with all its principles, throw all real values into the manure pit of mankind! What a fine and admirable example to leave to my children!"

It's important to know how a life begins, but it's even more important to know how one brings it to a close

Ercole's health was growing worse and worse, and by this point the physicians who were caring for him despaired of saving him. Talk in the city turned openly to the succession to the throne of the duchy.

When he heard about his father's condition, Alfonso hurried back to Ferrara on August 8. What brought him back to his homeland, aside from his desire to honor his dying father, was also his fear that his brothers might take advantage of his absence to attempt, with some coup or other, to push him aside and take power.

In the anteroom to the duke's bedchamber, Alfonso ran into Isabella, who had not left her father's bedside for several days now. Brother and sister rapidly embraced and Isabella started to say: "It's a good thing you've come back."

"How is he?" Alfonso asked, nodding his head toward the half-open bedroom door.

Isabella sighed. "His fever has been spiking, he can't stop shivering, it's horrible to see him like this."

"But is there no one staying with him?"

"Yes, Lucrezia never leaves him for a moment, she's been at his side for days now."

"I thank you for coming here all the way from Mantua to console him."

"Don't say that, he's my father. And believe me, I'm not sad to leave Mantua."

"Why do you say that?"

"Don't ask, let's just say that for a while now my husband has been a little too off-kilter, he can't seem to live with me or his children, he's a rude oaf."

Alfonso let a smile escape and answered: "You shouldn't take that the wrong way, he's probably just got a little too much of the rooster in him."

"What is that supposed to mean?"

"Why, you know what he's like, he's probably just infatuated with some all-too-willing young woman. I've never been too fond of your husband, to tell the truth, but these are innocent enough diversions, after all!"

Isabella fixed her brother with a contemptuous eye and muttered: "Perhaps, but evidently even the compliant girls he finds in the countryside are starting to bore him."

"What do you mean by that?"

"Nothing, nothing."

Alfonso took her hands in his: "Isabella, speak to me, since when do we have secrets from each other?"

"Forgive me," she said, cutting off the discussion, "I don't want to embitter you even more, in times like this we should only think about our father."

"Listen," he insisted, "there's no point in you letting whatever it is eat away at you like this, if our father were to notice it could even cause him harm . . . Come on, tell me everything and you'll feel better."

"Certainly it's hard to get a migratory bird to notice new things."

"Are you talking about me?"

"I most assuredly am."

"All right then. So tell me, what news is there?"

Isabella looked at him, took a deep breath, and began: "I don't know if I ought to, I don't know if it's right, but . . . have you already spoken with your wife?"

"No, I came here directly, why?"

"Spend as much time with her as you can. Listen to me, you see, Francesco . . . "

"Francesco what?" exclaimed Alfonso.

"Nothing, don't worry about it, nothing's happened, at least I don't think so . . . But it might be better for you if you weren't to give him too many opportunities, shall we say, to spend time with Lucrezia." Alfonso, livid with rage, grabbed her wrist and shouted: "Talk! Tell me everything immediately! What has that miserable wretch tried to do?"

"Please, Alfonso, stop it, you're hurting me! Let go of me, Lucrezia's right in the next room!"

He released her and then, in a very serious tone of voice, said again: "Tell me exactly what happened—everything!"

"I swear to you, nothing happened. Stop worrying and sit down."

Alfonso sat down and in an undertone asked: "So my wife is involved . . . You aren't hiding anything from me, are you?"

"No, I swear it. All I'm saying is that I think you should keep your eyes open. Stop spending so much time away from Ferrara."

Alfonso, turning to look at the door of the dying duke's bedroom, declared: "Unfortunately, Isabella, I have the impression that you won't see me in the flock of migrating birds ever again."

Just at that moment, Isabella took his hand and waved for him to stop speaking: Lucrezia had just emerged from the duke's bedroom. When she saw Alfonso sitting next to Isabella she let out a stifled cry and ran to him, throwing her arms around him.

"What a wonderful thing, that you've come back!"

"I felt the need for it myself," her husband replied, gazing at her with genuine affection.

Lucrezia looked at him tenderly and gave him a kiss, then said immediately: "Go, make haste, go to your father, but don't wake him up, please, he's just fallen asleep, he badly needs some rest."

Alfonso had an almost embarrassed expression on his face; Lucrezia gave him a light shove and walked him to the door.

"I'll wait for you in the garden," she said. He nodded and went in, closing the door behind him.

"Can I go with you?" Isabella asked her.

"Why of course! Come, a little fresh air will do us both a world of good."

The sisters-in-law went down a short staircase. Isabella put her weight on Lucrezia and asked her: "Help me for a moment, please, I've gotten so big that I'm having trouble walking."

"You need to get out more, some horseback riding for instance."

"Riding! What, on an elephant!? Look at my derriere: even an elephant would take fright!"

They both burst out laughing.

"You know," Lucrezia said with something close to a smile, "I always wondered what you and Alfonso must have been like as children, I've always been curious to hear you talk together, as a brother and sister . . . Just a moment ago I was about to open the door and I heard you talking, how sweet you were . . . And I also heard what you were saying about me."

Isabella looked at her, appalled, and hastened to say: "You heard us? I swear, Lucrezia, I . . . I only wanted to . . . I only said those things for his . . . For your good, for the two of you, but I assure you, I know perfectly well that . . . What I mean to say is that, Francesco . . . In other words, I know perfectly well that nothing happened . . . "

"I'm afraid you're wrong," Lucrezia said in a serious voice. "Something *has* happened."

Isabella stiffened: "What, where, when?"

"He spoke to me about his illness, or perhaps I should say, about his tragedy."

Isabella stood there for a moment, baffled, and then, almost in annoyance: "But why you? He's never talked about it with anyone else . . . ."

"I will tell you that ever since we've been working together on this matter of prisoners and trials, your husband and I have found ourselves confiding even very delicate matters to one another. Like that one. I confess that when he told me, I almost didn't believe him . . . And I even said to him: 'How could that be? You seem so healthy . . . ' I felt as if I'd been tipped head-first into a maelstrom of despair."

"Well, that's exactly how I felt when I found out. Suddenly I heard him raving like a lunatic . . . And I saw him stagger, lurch and reel like a filthy drunk, and I felt no pity for him, only hatred and contempt, because I couldn't forgive him for having gotten me pregnant even though he knew that by so doing he was endangering my life and the lives of my children."

"I can imagine what you must have experienced, my dear Isabella."

"No! Impossible! It's something you could never imagine!" And with these words she tore off the cape she was wearing and hurled it down onto the steps. "Look at me carefully, look at what I've become. When I heard that news I blew up like a foresail. Like a puffball. I put on ninety pounds! At home, I've had to move from the top floor to the ground floor, across from the stables, because I can no longer get up the stairs!"

At this point, we should provide a comment. In reading, or

perhaps we should say, in analyzing the countless things written about the Borgias but especially about Lucrezia, we have noticed one fundamental fact. None of these illustrious historians, and for that matter, out of all the writers who have composed obscene erotic accounts to drum up sales, none have focused on the central fact that Francesco Gonzaga was diseased with syphilis. En masse, these authors have sidestepped the problem or simply turned a blind eye. Syphilis: a marginal detail. How could that be? In those days it was well known that a man or a woman who made love with someone suffering from the lues venerea, as syphilis was known back then, was unlikely to emerge unharmed. There was an almost mathematical certainty that they would acquire that monstrous curse in their turn. And the same was true for their children. And in fact Federico, Francesco and Isabella's second son, contracted congenital lues, which is to say he inherited it from his father. How could Lucrezia, once she'd learned of the condition that afflicted Francesco, have agreed to become his lover? And what's more: how could she have then gone on to have five children in excellent health with her husband? It's the same old lie, and in the face of such a thing we have only one possible remedy: tell the story accurately, taking care not to betray the truth. Which is exactly what we are going to do.

The most painful farewell is when a wise man leaves you forever

In an atmosphere of intense melancholy, the people of Ferrara prepared for the loss of their duke. Ercole's condition steadily worsened: the man was seventy-four years old, and his few fleeting moments of lucidity were broken by extended fits of fever and the shakes.

A worried Alfonso was pacing the corridors of the castle

when he saw Lucrezia hurrying toward him at something close to a run.

"Hurry!" she said to him. "Your father wants to talk to the two of us, together."

Husband and wife hastily ran up the stairs that led to the duke's bedroom and entered, hand in hand. When Ercole saw his son, his face lit up in a broad smile of consolation and he waved for him to come closer. Alfonso sat down at his father's side and silently took his hand.

"My son," the duke began in a voice that was weary but happy, "at a time when you're about to lose your father, it is your duty to reflect on the gifts and graces that you have received. They are numerous, and one might safely say that no one has ever received such good fortune as you now possess. The important thing is for you to learn how to see it. It may seem unbelievable but sometimes the most wonderful things are also the ones we have the hardest time glimpsing. You have never understood, my son, the value of beauty, and yet beauty is the only thing that can truly save you in this world.

"You seem incapable of glimpsing the magnificence of a monument, a palace, or a cathedral, though happily there is still music which captures your soul. Indeed, when you are of a mind to, you can play beautifully, but you do nothing to cultivate that gift. And in the same way, you seem indifferent to the beauty of the woman that fortune has bestowed upon you: Lucrezia. And I'm not talking about the beauty of her hair, her face, and her body, I'm referring to the beauty that Lucrezia carries within her, a beauty that emanates. Her generosity, enthusiasm, passion, and willingness to make sacrifices for those she loves. I'd like to be a necromancer so that I could make you instantly see the enchantment that lies within this woman.

"And to you, Lucrezia, I say, do not abandon your judgment

to appearances. This son of mine, whom you will have to support in ruling this duchy, is like a linden tree covered with ivy, which masks its wonderful scent. It is easy to take that linden for a dead tree, good for nothing but firewood, but if you look at him, if you truly try to see him, you won't be able to keep yourself from loving him more deeply than you already do."

As Lucrezia and Alfonso listened to the duke's words, they were barely able to choke back their tears. They gazed into each other's eyes at considerable length.

Ercole lay in silence for a brief time, then, as if coming to, he whispered: "Now you both give me your hands and swear to me that you will love each other and help each other," and, after a moment, he added: "And that you'll take good care of this city of mine."

Alfonso burst into uncontrolled sobbing, his whole body shaking with his tears. Lucrezia took his hands and kissed them, stroking his hair. At last the duke's son managed to calm down and said to his father: "Father, I will keep your teachings forever in the trunk of my tree and I will make sure that they give bounteous fruit, for my own good, for that of my woman, and for the duchy. But allow me to give you a gift, so that I can begin to surround myself with the beauty of which you were speaking."

Having said that, he left the room for a moment and spoke a few words aside to a servant, while Lucrezia leaned over the duke and whispered to him: "*Grazie*, father, I promise I'll make him happy."

"I thank you, my daughter, and to think that I even took money to allow you to come live with us!" Laughing, he added: "You've been one of the greatest joys of my life."

Just then, the bedroom door flew open, followed instantly by the sound of song to the accompaniment of a viola. It was Alfonso playing.

Lucrezia and Ercole were enchanted. All the court musicians gathered around the bed and sang:

"Ohi, ma quand che morirò vojo veder tüta intorno zente che bala,
che dise cantando vaje tranquil.
Nessun planze per ti con la tristissia,
tu te ghe lassi dolze giojanza e cari regordi del too campar.
No se desmentega chi l'ha vissù de giostizia
e de plazer de viver feliz."

"Oh, when I die I want to see all around me people dancing,
saying in song go in tranquility.
No one weeps for you in sadness,
You who leave sweet joy and dear memories of your life."

Alfonso, setting down the viola from time to time, repeated the verses, singing them along with the musicians at the top of his lungs. Once the chorus was over, Ercole made a visible effort and hoisted himself up to a sitting position; he threw open his arms and his son rushed toward him and seized him in a hug. Lucrezia, visibly moved, watched this scene and when her husband stood up she literally threw herself into his arms. She pressed a long and passionate kiss on his lips and whispered: "You should have told me long ago that you too were a poet! Too bad I'm already married to you, otherwise in acknowledgment of this gift of music that you have given to your father and me, I'd immediately ask you to concede to me a first night of love with you."

A few days later, on January 25, 1505, Ercole's condition worsened and he died, attended to the very last by his daughter-in-law and his son.

In accordance with an ancient tradition, after the funeral,

the relatives repair together to consume a small meal of farewell to the departed, known as the "*pranzo d'addio per il defunto*," Lucrezia and Francesco Gonzaga climbed up to the second story of the Castello Vecchio of Ferrara. Isabella had asked if she could remain on the ground floor to spare herself the difficulty of climbing the stairs. Her brother Alfonso offered to keep her company. The two in-laws chose a few items of food and sat down at the long table, alone.

"My compliments, Duchess, at last you've done it."

"You're indulging in the usual heavy-handed sarcasm," Lucrezia replied. "Do you really think that wearing the ducal necklace was my chief objective?"

"No, I was just trying to get a rise out of you. I love to see your eyes when you're angry, they glitter and flash like lightning. But actually, seriously, I want you to think about the troubles that await you, now that the new duke, your husband, has reappointed you to the council on supplicants and amnesties, and you'll also have to attend to diplomatic relations with the most troublesome states, such as Venice, the French, the Spanish, and, above all, the pope. Let me warn you, and this is something that I know for sure, that it is this new pope Julius II's intention to eliminate the duchy of Ferrara as an independent state and annex it whole. And of course expel you all from this place."

"Thanks very much for the warning, but I've known that for a while now. I hope that when the pope actually attacks us you'll show how much you still care for us."

Writing notes about the things that happen to you is often a good way to remember only the good times

Lucrezia kept a diary in which she jotted down accounts of the various passages of her life. Here is a fragment that is of direct interest to us:

Today is Friday the seventh, and in my belly I felt a quiver growing. I'm sure of it, I'm pregnant. I feel tremendously happy, I shouted it out to my husband, leaning out over the huge plaza of the stables: 'We've done it, we're going to have a baby!'

Monday the twelfth. The plague that first broke out in the town of eels, Comacchio, is starting to reach Ferrara too. At dawn Alfonso had my bags packed, and to keep me from being jolted on the trip, since I'm close to my time to give birth, he loaded me onto a horse-drawn *bragozzo* which will take me by water to Guastalla, where a canal runs all the way to Reggio Emilia. There they'll meet me and take me to a safe place.

Tuesday, January 3, 1505. Yesterday there was an earthquake in Ferrara. A number of people were killed, many houses collapsed, and others are sure to fall with the next tremor. The entire populace has abandoned the city. There are more than four thousand refugees. This means that there is now no one in Ferrara, not even cats or stray dogs. Even our palace collapsed, but fortunately no one was caught inside. It's a remarkable thing, it was the very danger of the plague that saved me, my husband, and our baby from being crushed beneath all that rubble.

Saturday, September 19, 1505. This morning I had labor pains and then our son was born: a boy. Alfonso wasn't here, he had to go back to Ferrara to supervise the reconstruction of the ravaged city.

Saturday, September 26, 1505. Just a few days later, he's back at my side! I'm already up and about and I welcome him home with my baby clutched tight to my breast. We embrace, amidst cries of joy. Before long we realize that we are dancing to the tune of our kisses.

How often it is though that smiles dissolve into tears.

Little more than a month has gone by. I'm dissolving into

tears. Why have I been punished like this? Why did this baby of mine need to die? He hadn't yet learned to call me mamma.

Not long afterward, in Lucrezia's diaries, we find another entry. Here it is:

November 4, 1505. Yesterday Giulio, my husband's illegitimate half-brother, was attacked by a gang of thugs, among whom it is said was another of Alfonso's brothers, the Cardinal Ippolito d'Este. It is well known that both the cardinal and Giulio were in love with the same captivating damsel: Angela Borgia, my cousin. The day before yesterday she had confided to me that she preferred Giulio and she told me that Giulio's eyes alone were more beautiful than every inch of the cardinal. Ippolito apparently didn't take it well. As a result of that beating, poor Giulio was left bruised and broken and he even lost an eye. I asked my husband Alfonso to conduct an investigation to learn who the guilty parties were in this assault and punish them.

Further down, we read:

I feel as if I'd returned to Rome. I thought that I'd left that atmosphere of murders, conspiracies, and betrayals behind me, that I'd finally found an enlightened, civil place to live. Instead I see that men can be inhuman everywhere.

A woman who concedes no mitigating circumstances and reduces no sentences

But Lucrezia's expectations of her husband were destined for disappointment. In fact, given the fact that Ippolito was Alfonso's most important ally, her husband chose to whitewash the case and bury the file, circulating for public and semipublic consumption a version that completely omitted any reference whatsoever to the cardinal's involvement.

One night Duke Alfonso was descending the castle stairs on

his way to the stables when suddenly Lucrezia appeared before him and demanded, in an indignant voice: "Why did you twist and conceal the full truth?"

"What truth?" Alfonso asked in something close to resentment, and without grasping the point.

Lucrezia went on: "You allowed your brother Ippolito to attack Giulio with impunity, blinding him in one eye, for a personal vendetta, and all you did was stand by and watch! At first I couldn't bring myself to believe you'd ever be capable of such a thing, I trusted that you'd cleave to the values imparted to you by your father but instead you . . . you're just like my brother!" She began shouting: "Why do I always have to—"

Alfonso, terrified that Lucrezia's words might be overheard, grabbed her by the arm and dragged her into a nearby room.

"Never do such a thing again as long as you live," he lit into her aggressively. "Can you just imagine the scandal if someone had happened to hear you?"

Lucrezia replied incredulously: "The scandal! Your brothers are blinding each other and all you care about is the scandal!"

"Lucrezia, stop and listen to me, there are things that you couldn't possibly—"

"—understand?" she interrupted, finishing his sentence for him. "Believe me, I've been to a first-rate school of treachery and atrocities, and there are certain things that I understand perfectly. But what I still can't quite grasp is how a person can exploit even family ties for political ends and to gain power. Why don't you tell me how you brought yourself to stoop so low?"

Alfonso stared at her but could say nothing. Lucrezia in her turn looked at him and concluded, on her way out: "Take care, those who choose to take advantage and prefer their own interests through treachery and lies often destroy themselves and all trust with those they care for most."

*

Giulio partially recovered his sight, but he was still blinded by his thirst for revenge. In fact, the following year, with his brother Ferrante, he put together a conspiracy to murder Lucrezia's husband Alfonso and his brother Ippolito, but luckily the plot was unsuccessful. Ferrante was captured, though Giulio managed to flee to Mantua. But Francesco Gonzaga, unwilling to make an enemy of his brother-in-law by offering protection to someone who had made an attempt on Alfonso's life, agreed to hand him over, on the condition that the traitor's life would be spared. Giulio was led under the scaffold that had been erected in the courtyard of the castle of Ferrara, which was already thronged with people. Ferrante, his coconspirator, was on the scaffold, at the executioner's mercy. The envoy that Francesco had sent to accompany the prisoner handed over a letter to the duke. Alfonso tore open the seal, opened the letter, and read it aloud: "I herewith deliver into your hands your brother who tried to kill you, but I ask you to keep your word that you will not execute him."

Just then, Lucrezia appeared, sitting erect in the saddle of her horse, raising one hand in her husband's direction as if to let him know: "Here I am."

The duke immediately grasped the meaning of that gesture. In his turn, he lifted his hand in the executioner's direction and shouted: "Take them both to prison!" And then, speaking to the assembled populace: "The show is over, you can go home."

Bad news comes in bunches, just like grapes.
Sometimes they're bitter, most of the time, they're just rotten

A few months later Francesco, riding to town from Mantua, dismounted from his horse and went running up the staircase that led to the suite of the duchess of Ferrara, taking the steps three at a time. As he hurried into the vestibule he heard the sounds of shouts and exclamations coming from the great hall and recognized the voices of his brother- and sister-in-law.

He strode briskly into the room and said: "Sorry to disturb you, but I have some very important news for you."

Lucrezia replied in a joyful voice: "We know already, it's news from Spain, right?"

"Yes, I received it from the correspondent I sent there expressly at your behest."

Alfonso came over and asked: "Actually, I heard that he climbed out a window fifteen feet above the ground and fractured a foot and his shoulder. Has he recovered?"

"Yes, but . . . "

And Lucrezia replied: "But the important thing is that he survived!"

And Francesco: "There's a part of the news I have that I never would have wanted to have to tell you . . . ."

"Oh my God," said Lucrezia, "what's happened?"

Alfonso said: "We have heard that he's enlisted in the army of the king of Navarre, his brother-in-law."

And Lucrezia said: "Why should you be sorry, the profession of arms is the one that he's always followed!"

"Yes," Francesco replied, "but there was a battle, he was given command of the entire attacking army and during the siege of the city of Viana he was caught in an ambush . . . He's been killed."

Lucrezia started to scream but midway through her voice caught and failed, and she could no longer utter a sound. She shot a look of wild despair at both men and then fell into her husband's arms.

That very evening she went straight to the convent of Corpus Domini and for a whole week no one heard another thing about her.

Returning to Lucrezia's diary, we find the following entry:

April 5th, 1508. I find myself well beyond mere happiness and joy. Yesterday my and Alfonso's son was born. He's hale and healthy. The populace immediately gathered beneath the windows of the palace and shouted, as is traditional in all the regions of Romagna and Emilia: '*Ol è né 'o pà. Ercule ol sciame*,' 'Behold, the father is reborn! Ercole is his name.'

People with wit are being born in smaller and smaller numbers

A few months passed. All was calm and quiet when Francesco burst into Lucrezia's room like a madman and, without so much as saying hello, attacked her: "I told you, pleaded with you, not to go to that meeting armed with weapons to slice and pierce."

"Who on earth are you talking about?"

"Oh come on, don't pretend you were in some trance, that you weren't there, that you didn't know, and that maybe there was a brawl, but you didn't want it to happen, and it was all just an accident . . . "

"Sorry, but I still don't understand what you're talking about!"

"How can you fail to understand!? A man has been found stabbed with no fewer than twenty-two wounds. I can understand the passionate impetus that sweeps you Spaniards away, and I certainly realize you have a great deal of pent-up anger, but wasn't it enough to strike him good and hard five or six times? Why did you have to go overboard like that?"

"Listen, you're not funny in the slightest, so either explain matters or I'm going to have to leave. Now tell me, just who is this man who's been stabbed?!"

"Oh, all right, the murdered man is Ercole Strozzi."

"Who? The lame man?"

"That's right, the lame man, and they even found stab wounds on his lame leg, you really are insatiable!"

"When did this happen?"

"Last night."

"And do they know who did it?"

"How could they, if you say you don't?!"

"Listen, either you stop making fun of me, or I really will pull out a knife and I'll use it on you!"

"All right, all right, I was just kidding around . . . "

"Ah you were kidding around! Funny! You have an army general's sense of humor. So what you're telling me is that you made the whole thing up, including the murder of Strozzi?"

"No, unfortunately that is the one true thing, or actually not the only thing, since there's also the fact no one has any idea who could have killed him or who could have ordered it done . . . All right, well, enough said about that, I had actually come to give you some very important news: in a few months I'll be setting off for war again."

"You too?"

"What do you mean, me too?"

"My husband, just a short while ago, gave me the exact same news. What army are you going to command?"

"I'm going to be in the pope's army."

"You, on the pope's side? Weren't you supposed to be with the Venetians?"

"Please, don't say another word about my change of sides to a living soul, not even in passing! In fact, the adversary of the league now being formed is Venice: our aim is the total annihilation of the Serenissima."

"And for what reason? After all, they're only pursuing their own best interests, no different from what we're doing. Moreover the pope, very much like the Venetian Republic, still plans to gobble up all our lands in a single gulp, including Ferrara and Mantua."

"Of course, my dear, you wouldn't understand. Politics demands that the participants dance."

"What do you mean?"

"They must not stand still, not even for an instant. Today we are here, tomorrow we must be there, pardon, excuse me, would you care to dance? And remember that the watchword of all those allied in the league is this: peace. We are going to meet in Cambrai with but one objective: peace. How to keep the peace."

Pull out the meat grinder, then we distribute the pieces: whoever's fastest and most ruthless will get the choicest morsels

Now who were the members of this league, willing to stand in alliance? Here's the list: Louis XII of France; Maximilian I of Habsburg, the Holy Roman Emperor; Ferdinand II of Aragon, king of Naples and Sicily; Charles III, the Duke of Savoy. In short, all of Europe, if you count the latecomers Alfonso I d'Este and Francesco II Gonzaga.

They would divvy up among them Venice's dominions, including Dalmatia and the Mediterranean isles, up to and including Cyprus and Corfu. Each of them with their own choice tidbit, save Ferrara and Mantua. Those two realms took nothing away from the fight but their own survival.

Of the immense battle of Agnadello, also known as the battle of Chiara d'Adda, at which the Venetians were handed a resounding thumping by the troops under Alfonso's command, we have a truly remarkable eyewitness account. It comes to us from the author Angelo Beolco, whose pen name was Il Ruzzante, and who fought as a peasant soldier. Il Ruzzante tells the story of what happened and explains the real reasons leading to a vast massacre that marked the greatest defeat ever handed to the Serenissima in all its long history.

What could have brought together all those allied forces, that is, the League of Cambrai, and persuaded them to attack with such vehemence Venice, a sole city without allies?

You needn't look far: economic interests. The banks of Venice had invented the *maona*, that is, an early forerunner of the credit card. Any citizen of the Venetian Republic could buy what were in effect shares and thereby participate in the profits of one or several market operations, determined by the purchase of lands (in a territory that ranged from Dalmatia to Greece and then all the Mideast) or else by the armed conquest of the same. Yet the Serenissima rarely set out to conquer physically the territories it meant to exploit. More often Venice chose to leave the political governance to the local princes, while keeping for itself the fruit of those lands' resources paid as rent. This Venetian dominion was far more profitable than anything the other powers undertook, especially because they were underwritten by the tremendous economic power of Venice's banks, enterprises, and markets. Thanks to the direct involvement of the nascent entrepreneurial bourgeoisie, we can see that the whole affair was being managed not by a small elite of *possessores* but by a large and commercially active sector of the populace, a sector that was gradually and progressively expanding.

How to survive in a grotesque comedy, without a mask

In those years, at the very time when the states of the league, having laid low the Serenissima, were congratulating themselves over their stunning victory and were greedily preparing to loot the lands and wealth of the Venetian Republic, there was a theatrical troupe in Ferrara that was staging a very pointed commentary concerning the situation. It was one of the first companies of professional actors and it was

IMMAGINE DEL CONTADINO

Il Ruzzante

directed by no less a personage than Ludovico Ariosto, who ran the court theater. The company was staging a pantomime with musicians and comic performers that offered a grotesque parody of the truly chaotic situation into which much of Europe had fallen, with a succession of unexpected and often disastrous events.

During the production's prologue, jesters and clowns trooped onstage gussied up as ridiculous warriors, in costumes and masks, and they would fight ferociously, with the losers in those staged battles often lacerated and bruised. Of course, the trick in staging the massacre involved a quick and easy-to-miss switch, where real actors were replaced by mannequins.

As the production proceeded with its *danse macabre* that mixed the ghoulish with the grotesque, a new group of *Zanni*—the original term that gave us our word "zany"— would step into the limelight, dressed as street sweepers, pushing trash collectors' wheelbarrows and handcarts and, using pitchforks, they'd spear the scattered remains of the heroes who had been ripped to pieces. Then they'd toss them into the waiting receptacles, dancing all the while.

From the back of the stage came the victors, seated on thrones that were pushed by bishops and other high prelates. Here was the queen of France, dressed as a warrior in garb that was reminiscent of Joan of Arc. Immediately after her came the emperor Maximilian, holding in his hands a golden globe of the earth, which he tossed into the air at the exact instant that he caught another much larger one, hurled to him from off-stage. This marked the beginning of a display of juggling skills with a spectacular number of balls stuffed full of rags scattered in profusion across the stage. Among the jugglers was also the king of Spain, and at his side was Joanna the Mad, who amused herself by strolling the stage and spearing globes with an iron implement. Do you see the allegory?

During the grand finale of the production, the pontiff came

onstage, from the far end of the room. He wore a mask that reproduced a grotesque version of the face of Pope Julius II. When he made his entrance onto the stage, followed by his retinue of cardinals, the pope stepped up onto a dais, then threw open his mantle. Underneath, his warrior armor, with shield and sword, was visible. To accompany his benedictions he waved his sword, and behold, one after the other, his cardinals' heads were lopped clean off and their bodies went dancing cheerfully offstage, decapitated.

All the mimes and dancers pushed off to one side and at the center of the stage stood Joan of Arc, quite alone, representing France; she was given a number of enormous parchment scrolls, made of course with fake parchment. When the scrolls were unfurled, giant maps of all Lombardy appeared: Brescia, Bergamo, Crema, Cremona, and last but not least a large map of Milan. The holy warrior of France swallowed all those maps one by one, ripping them to shreds and every so often spitting out some particularly indigestible fragment. Little by little, as she tossed pieces of Lombard territory down her maw, she began to swell visibly in size, until her armor shattered into pieces. Immediately they dressed her in another suit of armor, and then another, until she was transformed into an enormous armed maiden who practically took up the whole stage. The other states of the gang tried to flee here and there until they were finally crushed against the walls by that all-devouring giantess.

The pope reemerged from the proscenium ditch that held the musicians. From the far end of the room, traveling over the heads of the audience, came a gondola. It was being rowed by the doge of Venice. The pope shouted:

"Most Serene Prince, the time has come for us to make peace if we both want to survive!"

"What are you saying, Holy Father? First you cut my throat," the doge shouted back, "and then you ask me to save you?"

And the pope replied: "Haven't you seen how large the Frankish queen has grown?"

"No, I don't trust you, first you take me to bed and then you treat me like some street-corner hooker. I want an honest wedding, in public, for one and all to see."

All at once, the scene shifts and we find ourselves at a banquet, a wedding feast. All the guests are seated before dishes piled high with food. Roast fowl, fried fish, cheese, fruit, and greens. The newlyweds rip food from each other's hands and even mouths. In the end the one who gets the most to eat is of course the pontiff, who grows visibly fatter and fatter. But then, alas, he explodes. Pieces of pope are everywhere. But from on high, in the blink of an eye, another pope descends, already gigantic to start with. The whole stage is filled with a vastly obese France that does its best to push its way through with its oversized belly. Likewise, Venice and the papacy charge into the fray with brutal belly-blows. In the end, exhausted by the fray, they collapse onto the boards and, with a sonorous chorus of snores, fall sound asleep.

Inside the time span of this pantomime, real-world events were happening that seemed as much a part of that absurd spectacle as anything else. Alfonso, now named commander of the league's troops, was forced to devote himself exclusively to the army and set aside his role in governing Ferrara. He therefore decided to entrust this very delicate and difficult task to the only person on whom he could rely completely, a person he considered singularly well prepared for the position, namely Lucrezia. And so she became the absolute regent of the duchy of Ferrara. For her, this was the apotheosis.

Shortly before the Battle of Chiara d'Adda, where our own Alfonso d'Este was preparing to direct the league's forces in one great attack, training vast quantities of cannon and spingardes, or breech-loading swivel guns, Francesco Gonzaga, who in turn held the office of high commander of the papal army, was suddenly seized by an especially severe onset of his disease. He would lose his senses and his balance, or be swept by fevers accompanied by violent tremors and partial paralysis of the legs. In brief, he was in no condition to command in battle. Word soon spread among the troops and with it unrest and mutiny among the captains and soldiers of the great armed corps. This development, as was to be expected, soon became fodder for slapstick and buffoonery in the hands of jesters in every city.

Some two months later, Francesco, now over his fit, found himself with a band of armed men crossing the boundary separating his own lands from the Venetian dominions, but he was unaware of the fact due to heavy fog. Almost immediately he encountered a squadron of Venetian infantry, who instantly recognized him and, to the cry of "There rides the traitor!" arrested him on the spot.

He was taken to Venice and there imprisoned in the Torretta. The marquis of Mantua thought that the Venetians might very well sentence him to death. He spent the days that followed in a state of considerable apprehension and physical discomfort, because the disease was especially virulent in such conditions. But Francesco guessed that the Serenissima planned only to hold him hostage until he could be ransomed at more advantageous terms. So he clenched his teeth and held out.

Isabella and Lucrezia both took immediate action, each of them independently sending words of entreaty to the Venetian Republic and offering terms that might lead to Francesco's liberation. Lucrezia went a step further and enlisted the aid of her husband who, lest we forget, was also the commander of the papal troops. He too actively tried to intercede on behalf of the noble prisoner.

Lucrezia knew that Isabella had fallen into a bottomless pit of despair and so she hurried to Mantua to comfort her. When she disembarked from the *bragozzo* as it tied up at the lakeside wharf, she found her friend waiting for her outside the castle's portal. Isabella immediately hurried toward her, though she moved with effort, and threw her arms around her: "I really needed to see a friendly face, and you're the only one who seems to be a true companion."

Once they'd entered the castle, naturally on the ground floor, the two women sat down to have lunch.

"What news do you have for me?"

"Would you mind very tactfully asking all the servants to leave us alone?"

"Right away, but why, what's happening?"

"Just a moment and you'll understand everything."

Isabella ordered all those who were present to leave the room and then asked: "Well, what is it?"

"You see, what I'm about to tell you is excellent news for your husband, but a serious problem if it happens to get out. By the way, are you quite certain that there are no indiscreet ears around, no one listening at doors or windows?"

"Don't worry, nobody's around."

"Fine. Now, you know that I have personally involved my own husband in the attempt to win the release of Francesco."

"Yes, I do know and I thank you. I also heard that Alfonso enjoys the pope's utmost respect and consideration, and that the pope considers him his most respected adviser."

"That's right, and that is where the good news comes in."

"Tell me, please tell me."

"The pope has confided in Alfonso, in the greatest secrecy, that he plans once again to modify the alliances."

"He wants to modify the alliances?"

"Hush, this is something that I should not even know, and neither should Alfonso. Apparently Pope Julius no longer considers Venice to be an especially grave threat."

"How could that be, if they're already divvying up the Venetian territories?"

"True, and yet at the same time they're preparing a new alliance with the doge."

"Seriously? From one day to the next? Today they're mortal enemies and tomorrow they become allies?"

Lucrezia smiled: "I've learned from experience that there is nothing so easy to change as a political alliance. But in this case, the advantage accrues to us."

"So what will become of this new array of forces?"

"I don't know, and it doesn't much matter right now. What does matter is that, when Venice and the pope are on the same side, we can be certain that your husband will be safe and free!"

Isabella, almost forgetting her physical difficulties, threw her arms around Lucrezia's neck: "You're my angel, Lucrezia!"

Everything was turning out for the best. The political about-face had been completed. Venice and the pope made peace. That wasn't all—they even formed an alliance. The prisoner was immediately released after a year behind bars, and he returned home battered but happy. Celebrations, hugs and kisses, singing into the night.

Suddenly, however, the fronts in the alliance switched direction. And that spelled a full-fledged disaster, especially for Ferrara. The pope, in fact, as stated, had decided to make peace with Venice, but at the same time—and this represented the new development—began to take steps to wage war on France. And so it was necessary to abandon the alliance with Louis XII, dissolve the League of Cambrai, and establish a new league, this time a holy league. This league would include the Germans and the Spanish. With God on their side.

Alfonso d'Este, gonfalonier of the pontiff's army, refused to turn his weapons against the French, who had always been staunch allies of his house. The pope therefore excommunicated him, effective immediately, and further decided to declare war on the duchy of Ferrara and bring it back under the sway of the church.

Paradox of paradoxes, the commander of the new papal forces called upon to attack Ferrara would be none other than the rehabilitated marquis of Mantua, Francesco Gonzaga, now risen to the rank of gonfalonier in Alfonso's place. Moreover, to ensure his continued loyalty to the pontiff, Francesco was obliged to hand over his ten-year-old son, Federico, as a hostage, the very son to whom he had, alas, transmitted the pox.

Alfonso had therefore decided to ally himself with the French forces and fight against the Holy League. As we have seen, in his absence Lucrezia governed Ferrara, and she displayed an impressive and clear-eyed determination. The duchess wrote more than one letter to her brother-in-law Francesco Gonzaga, who had suddenly and unexpectedly become an enemy, asking him to refrain to the best of his abilities from attacking the duchy of Ferrara.

Her first thought was for the safety of her children (the year previous she had given birth to another little boy, Ippolito), and she made plans to take them with her to Milan. But so great was the faith that the populace had in her that a huge crowd made its way to the castle, clamoring to be admitted to the four-sided portico. She came downstairs to stand in the midst of her Ferrarese and a spokesman for the crowd begged her not to abandon them.

"You are our only hope. With you we feel safe, but if you leave then we too will abandon the city."

Lucrezia took a deep breath and disguised her surge of emotion with a loud cough, saying: "After what you have done here, I'll never leave this city, for whatever reason. Unless our enemies capture me."

And so Lucrezia remained and helped to organize the defense of the city's walls. A new bastion was built, with the labor of both the city's women and its men.

It was her husband who was constantly at work supervising these operations, and she tells us a truly singular story about him. While he was standing on one of the ramparts supervising reinforcement of the defenses, an envoy from the pope arrived and handed him a papal bull. The duke tore open the envelope and read aloud for all to hear: "I, Julius II, pontiff of the Roman Ecclesia, order and command you to deliver the keys to the city into the hands of the envoy I have sent you; otherwise in a matter of days you will see the ammassed armies of the Holy See, the Spaniards, and the Germans arrive."

"Very well, tell the pope that he's convinced me. The minute I see his troops arriving, I'll arrange for him to receive the keys." Then Alfonso amicably locked arms with the envoy and walked with him to where he could easily point to an enormous cannon, already positioned and trained and ready to shoot. "Do you see that monstrous engine of destruction? We call it the *mazadiàvul*, the devil-killer. It doesn't fire stones, it shoots metal balls." So saying, he showed him one of those cannonballs: "Look, it's made of two sections, it's hollow inside, the two parts screw together, so all you have to do is unscrew it and it opens." He pulled a key from his pocket. "And what I'll do is put the key for the pontiff right there, I'll screw it shut, I'll put the ball into the mouth of the cannon and then *bang!* I'll shoot that key right into his arms, straight into His Holiness's belly. If His Holiness will be so good as to stand still, naturally."

Francesco Gonzaga, rendered incapable of leading the pope's army

At first they called it the "French pox," then the
"Spanish pox," and then in the sixteenth century they called it
"the general's medal"

But the pope simply refused to stay still. He had already reached Bologna, where he found the army led by Francesco. And so he told his general: "Well, then, get busy!"

"You'll have to forgive me, Your Holiness, it's not because I lack the courage or the determination, it's just that I'm so sick: I'm having recurring attacks of that disease that afflicts me. I'm taking mercury all day, I'm poisoning myself in an attempt to quieten the pain a little. And you, Holy Father, can understand better than most, since you caught the pox even before I did and you know the travails to which it puts a man."

The pontiff nodded: "I see your point. Get some rest, and when you feel strong enough, attack. But if there's one thing I want you to remember, it's this: say nothing about it! Nothing about your sickness, and nothing about mine!"

Meanwhile, in Ferrara, Lucrezia was chiefly concerned with bolstering the morale of the populace and welcoming her French allies with signs of gratitude and cordiality. She held parties for them in the city's squares and invited their captains to her palaces.

Concerning the welcome she gave the French, we still have a comment written by one of the most famous knights of the king of France, Pierre Terrail de Bayard, the legendary "knight without fear and beyond reproach," who said of her: "She was lovely and courteous and kind to one and all. I, who had the good fortune to know her personally, can safely say that she was a pearl in this world."

Practically by accident, on the plain of Ravenna, where as recently as a century ago there was still a muddy lake surrounding the five islands that made up that city, two armies clashed. There, on that day, the united forces of Ferrara and the French, with the aid of the artillery under Alfonso's command, defeated the troops of the league in the morass around Ravenna.

When the battle was over thousands of corpses littered the field: the dead of both sides. The French had lost their finest men, among them Gaston of Foix, the army's commander in chief; in Ravenna there is still a magnificent marble sculpture depicting the body, the armor, and the face of the dead warrior. For this reason the French troops decided to abandon the field and went back to Milan. And so the Ferrarese with their duke and duchess were left alone.

Alfonso, no longer capable of putting up any real opposition to the pope, went to Rome in a last-ditch effort to work out an agreement. The pope replied: "I'm willing to pardon you, but you must give up all your holdings."

"Give me just this one night to think it over. I will also need to compose a letter to inform my subjects."

Then he headed off to Palazzo San Clemente where he was staying as a guest, but halfway there he changed direction and galloped to Porta San Giovanni. There he ran into a funeral procession carrying the corpses of plague victims out of the city. He fell into line in that procession and galloped north without stopping for breath until he reached the Po.

Once the pope was informed of the duke's escape, he realized that he had been hookwinked. He ordered his troops to prepare to march north. Destination: Ferrara.

Alfonso took three months to reach his city, because he was forced to take the most tortuous routes to avoid the armed men the pope sent to track him down. And so he asked Fabrizio Colonna to escort him, and his guide led him through some truly out-of-the-way passes.

In the meanwhile, in Ferrara, once the news arrived that the terrible Swiss mercenaries were already on the march, the whole town leapt into action to ready its defenses. Once again it was Lucrezia who oversaw operations, as she waited for her husband to return; and once again it was she who bolstered the spirits of one and all with her calm and unruffled spirit.

Isabella watched anxiously and prayed for Ferrara and, in a letter she wrote to her brother, Cardinal Ippolito, she exclaimed: "The warrior pope expects all the possessions of the house of Este to fall into his hands, let God soon ruin him and make him die, as I hope He will."[6] As they say in Ferrara, God has a thousand ears and He always listens with His good ear. Sure enough, the pope had one final fit and died. The news reached Ferrara with unbelievable speed, and the populace broke out into shouts, dances, and undescribable celebrations.

That pope whom we saw descend from on high in the grotesque pantomime was Julius II's successor, Leo X, the son of Lorenzo de' Medici. And it was precisely as in the finale of the pantomime that we described to you that Pope Julius II—Giuliano della Rovere—who we know planned to take back the city of Ferrara with all its possesions, finally gave up the ghost and returned to his maker.

The whole populace of Ferrara celebrated with a carnivalesque funeral their enemy the pope's descent into hell. At the same time, they cheered the new pontiff, who had shown himself to be favorable to the house of Este. Behind him was an individual we know very well, who persuaded him to change papal policies toward the duchy. This of course was Pietro Bembo, who had become the Holy Father's private secretary. This truly was a surprise, because we remember him as reluctant to don the garb of a politician; but later we will be absolutely gobsmacked to see him don a cardinal's tunic and vestments.

[6] Ibidem.

What's the fun of being rich if you don't have poor people around to pity?

It was in that period that Lucrezia decided to establish the first Monte di Pietà (or "mount of piety," an institutional pawnbroker common throughout Europe from the late Middle Ages on) in Ferrara, in order to provide succor for the city's indigent and the paupers of the surrounding countryside. What could have led the woman, who by now everyone called the "kind duchess," to establish at that precise moment an institution offering eleventh-hour salvation to the poor?

The incessant warring had brought disaster to the Po valley: fields were devastated by the armies, which forced peasants to abandon their lands and created shortages of grains and vegetables even in the city markets. As always, when there was a crisis, the usurers showed up, thriving in that climate and infecting every angle of life. But Lucrezia's plan was certainly not to found a lending institution like the banks that had sprung up in nearly all the cities, offering money at rates less brutal than the common usurers, but still the cause of horrifying collective disasters.

In fact, right at the end of the fifteenth century, the most important bank on the Italian peninsula, the Banco dei Medici, collapsed in Florence. The disaster affected the small merchants, artisans, and shopkeepers with especial violence, but its consequences rippled out to hurt all poor people. Those who were unable to pay the rent on their houses were forced to abandon them and leave the city.

And so, as Lucrezia returned to Ferrara—and let us not forget, she was still the repository of all its suppliants—she found herself presented with piles of requests for her intervention to save struggling citizens. Whatever could have led her to come up with the idea of organizing such a complex institution, and one that would prove so onerous to the coffers of the city's government?

There can be little doubt that some inspiration came from the writings of a genuine innovator of his time, Fra Bernardino of Siena, whose sermons were gathered and printed in the vernacular while the holy man was still alive. It is likely that Lucrezia came into possession of those writings when she took refuge in the convent after her forced separation from her first husband, Francesco Sforza.

The chief themes of Bernardino's message had little to do with the generic doctrinal topics of so much preaching being done then. Instead they concerned matters of economics and the problems of markets and survival. Incredibly, he was the author of a book entitled *Sui contratti e l'usura* (*On Contracts and Usury*). In this text, the monk ventured passionately into the problems of private property, speculation, and the exploitation of labor. One almost begins to wonder if Marx copied from him. His sermons not only touched on matters of speculation and loan-sharking; he also addressed a phenomenon that had spread so widely that it was causing serious damage to the society of his times. The matter in question was gambling. These fully fledged machines for despoiling honest citizens were not only run by gangs of criminals; even state governments, including the Vatican, procured significant income streams by running lotteries and other systems for collective betting.

And so, as absurd as it may seem, Bernardino was put on trial for heresy. The main charge was that he had declared money, including that coined by the pope, a tool of the devil. Luckily for him, the trial ended in his acquittal.

Lucrezia first composed a *grida*, or edict, and then hired a substantial number of town criers to read that text aloud during the markets and, with the bishop's approval, in the town's churches during services as well. Here's what the people heard: "For years a great number of infamous rogues have been working in this city, practicing the trade of usury, or, if you prefer the term, loan-sharking. The plague itself is less of a monstrous scourge than the lending of money at prohibitive rates of interest. Whole families have been ruined by these criminals, who offer cash at rates of up to thirty percent, only to increase those rates every time you miss a payment. We, with this new charitable bank of ours, aim to take their place, not in order to lay our hands on your money, but to keep these thieves from laying their hands on it. Consider that for years now in Venice these despicable loan-sharks have been punished by being placed in the pillory, hung out for days at a time in the iron cage at the tower of justice, and then stripped of the rights of citizenship and banished from the city forever. Well, we now announce to these miserable miscreants that from this day forth the same law will apply in Ferrara. With this goal in mind we have created a special gendarmerie that has already provided us with the names of the wrongdoers, some of whom are languishing in prison as we write. Through this newly founded bank we will accept anyone's requests for loans. Have no fear that your need will be classified as unworthy; you will not be required to offer any collateral. In exchange, however, you will be required to perform certain services for the public good for a certain number of days every week until your debt has been paid off."

But where did Lucrezia get the idea for this *grida*? In all likelihood precisely from one of those *concioni*, or speeches, that St. Bernardino delivered to the assembled public in the piazzas of Siena a hundred years earlier and which were being republished in those very same years.

Where did this revolutionary, to say the least, monk come from? The saint took many of his ideas in turn from Catherine of Siena, who had preached those notions before him in the very *contrade,* or quarters, of Siena, the city of the Palio. When she was still quite young, she joined the community of the

Mantellate. At this point, she had an encounter more or less similar to that of St. Francis. She happened to provide succor to a leper, and from there it became clear to her that the path she should follow was to devote herself to the poor and sick.

During the numerous epidemics, the issue of giving care to the sick became a stark struggle. Catherine managed to involve a considerable number of young men and women, and formed the so-called "Bella Brigata," or band of beauties. These volunteers transformed themselves into veritable flocks of festive young people who gave care to the needy. Hence their playful nickname. And it all sprang from the atmosphere that this young woman was able to create around herself.

It is enough to read a few lines from the letters that she dictated to her followers to get a stunning sense of her unusual language: "It is not hard to remain in the holy love of God. Sweet Jesus. Jesus is love. Those among us who are able to live in the overwhelming awareness of our brief time in this world, as brief as a pinpoint tossed in the wind, will seek neither honors nor power nor grandeur; nor wealth will they possesss through greed: and if they do have riches, they will become dispensers of Christ to the poor."

This way she had of expressing herself, at once simple and poetic, managed to astonish and move even men of great learning and vast power, such as Bernabò Visconti for instance, as well as bishops and even popes, toward whom she showed absolutely no shyness or intimidation.

"What are you doing up north in Avignon?" Catherine wrote to the pontiff. "Your see has been in Rome for centuries and you've left it vacant. For what reason? What benefit does the church gain thereby? Was it perhaps up north in Provence that Peter the fisherman first cast his nets? Was it there that he had himself nailed upside down to the cross, lest he copy the sacrifice of Christ? One day, if you have the time, you'll have to explain to me why you moved to Avignon, followed by such a vast crowd of bankers that they outnumbered the bishops who accompanied you."

When she arrived in Ferrara, Lucrezia brought with her not only the sermons of Bernardino, now a saint, but also the letters of St. Catherine that she had managed to gather in the convents of Rome. These writings, from the very beginning of her life, would be the crucial keys to her way of thinking and acting. Through her example, she succeeded in influencing part of the court, and especially Alfonso, with whom she managed to establish a relationship of authentic love.

In the name of St. Bernardino and inspired by the ideas of St. Catherine she would even found a convent of Dominican sisters. But she took great care not to found a sort of house of mortification dedicated exclusively to contrition and prayer where women would gather in collective rejection of everything that could distract them from religious contemplation.

And with St. Bernardino, she continued to repeat: "Everything that is festive comes from God and cannot be sinful; it is the exaltation of nature itself." There was more: "The greatest gift that you can give to Christ is the act of giving, not receiving."

On the ninth anniversary of the foundation of the convent, the conversas and the elder nuns invited Lucrezia to deliver a speech that would long be remembered in that house and by all those sisters.

She said: "We have not built this place, wrapping it in strong walls, to protect from the physical and moral dangers of the world but rather, as St. Catherine says, in order to open ourselves to the world, and to let love live and fulfill itself in us. Love not only toward God but toward every creature that needs it.

"Love is the Creator's greatest invention and, as St. Ambrose said, that is especially true when our entire spirit and body are involved in this extraordinary rite, which is after all the rite of our own birth and of our descent.

"My beloved sisters, I wish to tell you that a few weeks ago I had a baby, a tiny daughter, who proved to be happy and healthy. I hoped that I too would share her miraculous energy. But the contrary happened. I must yield to nature. Perhaps not immediately, since in this moment my pain has somewhat subsided. But I know that it will return. Our most clement Creator has given me so many gifts that I can see the end of my life and feel that within a few hours I shall be done with it. I recommend to your prayers my spouse and my children. And to you I hope that this life will make you think festively of the wonder of being alive."

Lucrezia

BIBLIOGRAPHY

Various Authors, *Lucrezia Borgia. Storia e mito*, Leo S. Olschki Editore, Florence 2006.

Pietro Bembo, Lucrezia Borgia, *La grande fiamma. Lettere 1503-1517*, Archinto, Milan 1989.

Sarah Bradford, *Lucrezia Borgia: Life, Love, and Death in Renaissance Italy*, Viking, New York 2004.

Geneviève Chastenet, *Lucrezia Borgia. La perfida innocente*, Mondadori, Milan 1995.

Alexandre Dumas, *I Borgia*, Sellerio, Palermo 2004.

Roberto Gervaso, *I Borgia*, Rizzoli, Milan 1980.

Ferdinand Gregorovius, *Lucretia Borgia*, Appleton, New York 1904.

Marion Johnson, *The Borgias*, Penguin, London 1981.

Special thanks go to the Biblioteca Malatestiana in Cesena and the Biblioteca Comunale "Aurelio Saffi" in Forlì.

About the Author

Born near Lago Maggiore in Italy in 1926, Dario Fo is an actor, playwright, comedian, director, songwriter and political campaigner. His first one-act was produced in 1958 and since then he has written, directed and acted in over forty plays and theatrical productions. In 1997 he was awarded the Nobel Prize for Literature. In the words of the Nobel Prize committee: "He if anyone merits the epithet of jester in the true meaning of that word. With a blend of laughter and gravity he opens our eyes to abuses and injustices in society and also the wider historical perspective in which they can be placed." *The Pope's Daughter* is his first novel.

EUROPA EDITIONS BACKLIST
(alphabetical by author)

Fiction

Carmine Abate
Between Two Seas • 978-1-933372-40-2 • Territories: World
The Homecoming Party • 978-1-933372-83-9 • Territories: World

Milena Agus
From the Land of the Moon • 978-1-60945-001-4 • Ebook • Territories: World (excl. ANZ)

Salwa Al Neimi
The Proof of the Honey • 978-1-933372-68-6 • Ebook • Territories: World (excl UK)

Simonetta Agnello Hornby
The Nun • 978-1-60945-062-5 • Territories: World

Daniel Arsand
Lovers • 978-1-60945-071-7 • Ebook • Territories: World

Jenn Ashworth
A Kind of Intimacy • 978-1-933372-86-0 • Territories: US & Can

Beryl Bainbridge
The Girl in the Polka Dot Dress • 978-1-60945-056-4 • Ebook • Territories: US

Muriel Barbery
The Elegance of the Hedgehog • 978-1-933372-60-0 • Ebook • Territories: World (excl. UK & EU)
Gourmet Rhapsody • 978-1-933372-95-2 • Ebook • Territories: World (excl. UK & EU)

Stefano Benni
Margherita Dolce Vita • 978-1-933372-20-4 • Territories: World
Timeskipper • 978-1-933372-44-0 • Territories: World

Romano Bilenchi
The Chill • 978-1-933372-90-7 • Territories: World

Kazimierz Brandys
Rondo • 978-1-60945-004-5 • Territories: World

Alina Bronsky
Broken Glass Park • 978-1-933372-96-9 • Ebook • Territories: World
The Hottest Dishes of the Tartar Cuisine • 978-1-60945-006-9 • Ebook •
Territories: World

Jesse Browner
Everything Happens Today • 978-1-60945-051-9 • Ebook • Territories:
World (excl. UK & EU)

Francisco Coloane
Tierra del Fuego • 978-1-933372-63-1 • Ebook • Territories: World

Rebecca Connell
The Art of Losing • 978-1-933372-78-5 • Territories: US

Laurence Cossé
A Novel Bookstore • 978-1-933372-82-2 • Ebook • Territories: World
An Accident in August • 978-1-60945-049-6 • Territories: World (excl. UK)

Diego De Silva
I Hadn't Understood • 978-1-60945-065-6 • Territories: World

Shashi Deshpande
The Dark Holds No Terrors • 978-1-933372-67-9 • Territories: US

Steve Erickson
Zeroville • 978-1-933372-39-6 • Territories: US & Can
These Dreams of You • 978-1-60945-063-2 • Territories: US & Can

Elena Ferrante
The Days of Abandonment • 978-1-933372-00-6 • Ebook • Territories: World
Troubling Love • 978-1-933372-16-7 • Territories: World
The Lost Daughter • 978-1-933372-42-6 • Territories: World

Linda Ferri
Cecilia • 978-1-933372-87-7 • Territories: World

Damon Galgut
In a Strange Room • 978-1-60945-011-3 • Ebook • Territories: USA

Santiago Gamboa
Necropolis • 978-1-60945-073-1 • Ebook • Territories: World

Jane Gardam
Old Filth • 978-1-933372-13-6 • Ebook • Territories: US
The Queen of the Tambourine • 978-1-933372-36-5 • Ebook • Territories: US
The People on Privilege Hill • 978-1-933372-56-3 • Ebook • Territories: US
The Man in the Wooden Hat • 978-1-933372-89-1 • Ebook • Territories: US
God on the Rocks • 978-1-933372-76-1 • Ebook • Territories: US
Crusoe's Daughter • 978-1-60945-069-4 • Ebook • Territories: US

Anna Gavalda
French Leave • 978-1-60945-005-2 • Ebook • Territories: US & Can

Seth Greenland
The Angry Buddhist • 978-1-60945-068-7 • Ebook • Territories: World

Katharina Hacker
The Have-Nots • 978-1-933372-41-9 • Territories: World (excl. India)

Patrick Hamilton
Hangover Square • 978-1-933372-06-8 • Territories: US & Can

James Hamilton-Paterson
Cooking with Fernet Branca • 978-1-933372-01-3 • Territories: US
Amazing Disgrace • 978-1-933372-19-8 • Territories: US
Rancid Pansies • 978-1-933372-62-4 • Territories: USA

Alfred Hayes
The Girl on the Via Flaminia • 978-1-933372-24-2 • Ebook •
Territories: World

Jean-Claude Izzo
The Lost Sailors • 978-1-933372-35-8 • Territories: World
A Sun for the Dying • 978-1-933372-59-4 • Territories: World

Gail Jones
Sorry • 978-1-933372-55-6 • Territories: US & Can

Ioanna Karystiani
The Jasmine Isle • 978-1-933372-10-5 • Territories: World
Swell • 978-1-933372-98-3 • Territories: World

Peter Kocan
Fresh Fields • 978-1-933372-29-7 • Territories: US, EU & Can
The Treatment and the Cure • 978-1-933372-45-7 • Territories: US, EU & Can

Helmut Krausser
Eros • 978-1-933372-58-7 • Territories: World

Amara Lakhous
Clash of Civilizations Over an Elevator in Piazza Vittorio •
978-1-933372-61-7 • Ebook • Territories: World
Divorce Islamic Style • 978-1-60945-066-3 • Ebook • Territories: World

Lia Levi
The Jewish Husband • 978-1-933372-93-8 • Territories: World

Valerio Massimo Manfredi
The Ides of March • 978-1-933372-99-0 • Territories: US

Leïla Marouane
The Sexual Life of an Islamist in Paris • 978-1-933372-85-3 •
Territories: World

Lorenzo Mediano
The Frost on His Shoulders • 978-1-60945-072-4 • Ebook •
Territories: World

Sélim Nassib
I Loved You for Your Voice • 978-1-933372-07-5 • Territories: World
The Palestinian Lover • 978-1-933372-23-5 • Territories: World

Amélie Nothomb
Tokyo Fiancée • 978-1-933372-64-8 • Territories: US & Can
Hygiene and the Assassin • 978-1-933372-77-8 • Ebook • Territories: US & Can

Valeria Parrella
For Grace Received • 978-1-933372-94-5 • Territories: World

Alessandro Piperno
The Worst Intentions • 978-1-933372-33-4 • Territories: World
Persecution • 978-1-60945-074-8 • Ebook • Territories: World

Lorcan Roche
The Companion • 978-1-933372-84-6 • Territories: World

Boualem Sansal
The German Mujahid • 978-1-933372-92-1 • Ebook • Territories: US & Can

Eric-Emmanuel Schmitt
The Most Beautiful Book in the World • 978-1-933372-74-7 • Ebook •
Territories: World
The Woman with the Bouquet • 978-1-933372-81-5 • Ebook • Territories:
US & Can

Angelika Schrobsdorff
You Are Not Like Other Mothers • 978-1-60945-075-5 • Ebook •
Territories: World

Audrey Schulman
Three Weeks in December • 978-1-60945-064-9 • Ebook • Territories: US
& Can

James Scudamore
Heliopolis • 978-1-933372-73-0 • Ebook • Territories: US

Luis Sepúlveda
The Shadow of What We Were • 978-1-60945-002-1 • Ebook • Territories:
World

Paolo Sorrentino
Everybody's Right • 978-1-60945-052-6 • Ebook • Territories: US & Can

Domenico Starnone
First Execution • 978-1-933372-66-2 • Territories: World

Henry Sutton
Get Me out of Here • 978-1-60945-007-6 • Ebook • Territories: US & Can

Chad Taylor
Departure Lounge • 978-1-933372-09-9 • Territories: US, EU & Can

Roma Tearne
Mosquito • 978-1-933372-57-0 • Territories: US & Can
Bone China • 978-1-933372-75-4 • Territories: US

André Carl van der Merwe
Moffie • 978-1-60945-050-2 • Ebook • Territories: World
(excl. S. Africa)

Fay Weldon
Chalcot Crescent • 978-1-933372-79-2 • Territories: US

Anne Wiazemsky
My Berlin Child • 978-1-60945-003-8 • Territories: US & Can

Jonathan Yardley
Second Reading • 978-1-60945-008-3 • Ebook • Territories: US & Can

Edwin M. Yoder Jr.
Lions at Lamb House • 978-1-933372-34-1 • Territories: World

Michele Zackheim
Broken Colors • 978-1-933372-37-2 • Territories: World

Alice Zeniter
Take This Man • 978-1-60945-053-3 • Territories: World

Tonga Books

Ian Holding
Of Beasts and Beings • 978-1-60945-054-0 • Ebook • Territories: US & Can

Sara Levine
Treasure Island!!! • 978-0-14043-768-3 • Ebook • Territories: World

Alexander Maksik
You Deserve Nothing • 978-1-60945-048-9 • Ebook • Territories: US, Can & EU (excl. UK)

Thad Ziolkowski
Wichita • 978-1-60945-070-0 • Ebook • Territories: World

Crime/Noir

Massimo Carlotto
The Goodbye Kiss • 978-1-933372-05-1 • Ebook • Territories: World
Death's Dark Abyss • 978-1-933372-18-1 • Ebook • Territories: World
The Fugitive • 978-1-933372-25-9 • Ebook • Territories: World
Bandit Love • 978-1-933372-80-8 • Ebook • Territories: World
Poisonville • 978-1-933372-91-4 • Ebook • Territories: World

Giancarlo De Cataldo
The Father and the Foreigner • 978-1-933372-72-3 • Territories: World

Caryl Férey
Zulu • 978-1-933372-88-4 • Ebook • Territories: World (excl. UK & EU)
Utu • 978-1-60945-055-7 • Ebook • Territories: World (excl. UK & EU)

Alicia Giménez-Bartlett
Dog Day • 978-1-933372-14-3 • Territories: US & Can
Prime Time Suspect • 978-1-933372-31-0 • Territories: US & Can
Death Rites • 978-1-933372-54-9 • Territories: US & Can

Jean-Claude Izzo
Total Chaos • 978-1-933372-04-4 • Territories: US & Can
Chourmo • 978-1-933372-17-4 • Territories: US & Can
Solea • 978-1-933372-30-3 • Territories: US & Can

Matthew F. Jones
Boot Tracks • 978-1-933372-11-2 • Territories: US & Can

Gene Kerrigan
The Midnight Choir • 978-1-933372-26-6 • Territories: US & Can
Little Criminals • 978-1-933372-43-3 • Territories: US & Can

Carlo Lucarelli
Carte Blanche • 978-1-933372-15-0 • Territories: World
The Damned Season • 978-1-933372-27-3 • Territories: World
Via delle Oche • 978-1-933372-53-2 • Territories: World

Edna Mazya
Love Burns • 978-1-933372-08-2 • Territories: World (excl. ANZ)

Yishai Sarid
Limassol • 978-1-60945-000-7 • Ebook • Territories: World (excl. UK, AUS & India)

Joel Stone
The Jerusalem File • 978-1-933372-65-5 • Ebook • Territories: World

Benjamin Tammuz
Minotaur • 978-1-933372-02-0 • Ebook • Territories: World

Non-fiction

Alberto Angela
A Day in the Life of Ancient Rome • 978-1-933372-71-6 • Territories: World • History

Helmut Dubiel
Deep In the Brain: Living with Parkinson's Disease • 978-1-933372-70-9 •
Ebook • Territories: World • Medicine/Memoir

James Hamilton-Paterson
Seven-Tenths: The Sea and Its Thresholds • 978-1-933372-69-3 • Territories:
USA • Nature/Essays

Daniele Mastrogiacomo
Days of Fear • 978-1-933372-97-6 • Ebook • Territories: World • Current
affairs/Memoir/Afghanistan/Journalism

Valery Panyushkin
Twelve Who Don't Agree • 978-1-60945-010-6 • Ebook • Territories:
World • Current affairs/Memoir/Russia/Journalism

Christa Wolf
One Day a Year: 1960-2000 • 978-1-933372-22-8 • Territories: World •
Memoir/History/20th Century

Children's Illustrated Fiction

Altan
Here Comes Timpa • 978-1-933372-28-0 • Territories: World (excl. Italy)
Timpa Goes to the Sea • 978-1-933372-32-7 • Territories: World (excl. Italy)
Fairy Tale Timpa • 978-1-933372-38-9 • Territories: World (excl. Italy)

Wolf Erlbruch
The Big Question • 978-1-933372-03-7 • Territories: US & Can
The Miracle of the Bears • 978-1-933372-21-1 • Territories: US & Can
(with **Gioconda Belli**) *The Butterfly Workshop* • 978-1-933372-12-9 •
Territories: US & Can